A VAMPIRE QUEEN'S DIARY
BOOK 2

CAMAZOTZ

by
P. A. HARRELL

# CAMAZOTZ

Camazotz personifies death, sacrifice and people greatly fear the caves that are thought to be his lair. In Mayan Mythology, this evil mythical creature was a gigantic vampire bat said to be the same size as a full grown human male, sometimes even much larger with the body of a man and the head of a bat.. But to me he is my one true love who stole my heart all those years ago. I do not care what anyone thinks of him, for I am his as he is mine!

# ACKNOWLEDGEMENTS

I would like to thank my loving husband Randy Camaz" for this wonderful life or death depending On how you look at it. Oh how how you makes my heart sing with joy! I would like to thank my three best friends "Lisa",Marylou and Lissa, "for standing by me while I was composing my diary. Ladies you are the best friends a vampire queen could every ask for. I would also like to thank all of my family and friends who have stood by me through thick and thin making this second book possible. I love you all!

# PROLOGUE

The vampire that has our daughter speaks, "If she means that much to you both then have your wife come to me of her own free will!" I start to walk toward him but Camaz stops me saying, "No you cannot do this, you do not understand what he is asking of you. If you go to him of your own free will that will break our bond and you will be his!" I look into his eyes and say, "You are my one true love and soul mate, I will love you for all of eternity, but I cannot allow harm to come to our daughter!" I say to the vampire, "I agree to your terms, now release my daughter!" At that moment I felt something snap within me. I felt all alone, as if Camaz had left me.

## CHAPTER 1

## THE CHASE

As we look down from above we spot our prey leaving a local bar. They have had quite a lot to drink and are staggering down the street. I say to Camaz, "Look at those fools! They can hardly walk!" He Laughs saying, "So I see. Should we give them a lift?" "Sounds good to me!" So we leap from the Building and land behind the two men. We walk up grabbing them from behind, shoot straight up into the air and fly off toward the woods, they are so startled they cannot even move. We land in An open field and drop them to the ground. They stare up at us in disbelief. Then one man speaks, "What the hell are you and why did you bring us here?" I laugh saying, "Well, my good sir, we are vampires and we brought you here for a hunt. We are going to give you a fifteen minute head start, then we are going to hunt you down and drain the blood from you bodies!" He stares at me opened mouthed. I smile at him baring my fangs for him to see. He screams and takes off running, the other is right on his heels. I walk to where Camaz is standing, look up at him, smile and say, "Don't you just love a good chase!" He chuckles, "Oh yes my dear I sure do, so what do you want to do for fifteen minutes?" I smile at him,"Oh I don't know, what do you think about some heavy petting? We can finish at home after our meal." He smiles at me, takes me in his arms and begins to kiss me slowly. I think, "Oh goodie, let the petting begin!" Fifteen minutes later we begin our hunt. One man has gone to the left the other to the right. I start to go off to the right but Camaz stops me, "No I will not have you going off with out me." "But Camaz if we both go after just one the other one will get away." "I know, dear heart, but I will not have you going after him alone. We will get the first, then the other. He will not get away." So we take off after the man that ran to the right. We catch up to him within minutes. I leap at him taking him down to the ground. He is screaming at the top of his lungs. I slam his head to the side and strike. His sweet salty blood begins to run down my throat quenching my burning thirst, I have him drained quickly. We then take to the air in search of the other man, we pick up on his scent several miles away. Camaz swoops down on him knocking him to the ground. I have landed right beside him and watch my man work, I love watching him feed, it turns me on! He looks up from his prey and asks, "Did you have something in mind dear, I know that look on you face!" I laugh and say, " You know how horny it makes me watching you feed! Let's go home!!" We take to the air and head back to the castle, when we arrive the family is still up. Kim comes running to me and says, "I have great news, there is going to be a double wedding Daniel and Dempie are both getting married!" I smile, "That is great news, when will the wedding be?" She tells me they will all be arriving in two weeks and the wedding will be in a month. Planning starts tomorrow for our double wedding. Two weeks later the boys arrived with their future brides. Daniel's girl is named Sabrina and she is an Irish princess. Dempie's girl is Veronica she is a human from America. They had fallen in love. He revealed himself to her. She said it did not matter she wanted to spend the rest of her life with him. Veronica's transformation is planned for three days before the wedding. As with Kim, Camaz will perform the transformation. We have readied everything in the guest room for her change. Veronica arrived the following evening. She is quite lovely with long blonde hair and baby blue eyes. She is about my height and build. She looked so scared. I invited her for a talk down in our quarters. She sat down on the bed next to me, I took her hand, "I know you are frightened, child. But it will be over in two days and you will open your eyes to a brand new life! For you see, I was like you once, I was made vampire in 1974 by my loving husband. We have been together since." She gave me a small smile and asked, "Where you not afraid of the change?" "Yes, my dear, at first I was. But Camaz stayed by my side the whole time reassuring me everything was going to be alright. Then at the end of the two days I opened my eyes to this wondrous life and never looked back!" I told her everything that was going to happen during the change and that we all would be there for her. The following evening she had prepared herself and smiled at Dempie, and said, "My darling I do this for you, so we can spend eternity together!" He kisses her gently on the lips. Camaz comes to her and explains what he is about to do. She turns her head exposing her neck to him. Like a snake, he strikes then recoils just as quick, leaving the gene behind,her burning began Veronica burned for a little over two days screaming for death the whole time. But we were all there for her. Dempie sat beside her on the bed, holding her hand and talking to her in a soothing voice. When her heart took it's final beat she opened her eyes to our life. She smiled up at Dempie and said, "I love you!" He took her in his arms and kissed her passionately. They left shortly after so her training could begin. We have much to do tonight as the double wedding is tomorrow evening. But first we hunt, I am starving!

## CHAPTER 2

## THE GREAT DOUBLE WEDDING

The following evening as I was getting dressed for the wedding Camaz came up to me, kissed me on my shoulder and told me how beautiful I looked. I had chosen a strapless gown in pale lavender. The top was beaded in pearls and the bottom flowed to the floor in waves. I had chosen to wear my diamond tiara and matching jewelery. I handed my necklace to Camaz and ask him to latch it around my neck, I then raised my long hair away from my neck. He clasp the necklace then turned me around to him, taking me into his arms. He then said, "You are my life! I would do anything for you including laying down my life for you!" He pulls me to his lips kissing me tenderly. I break the kiss and whisper, "Later my love we have a wedding to attend!" He laughs at my comment saying, "As you wish my queen but we will take this up again later!" He escorts me down to the great hall, there are many in attendance for the wedding. My best friends Louisa and Marylou arrived yesterday with their husbands. Both boys are standing at the alter awaiting their brides. Sabrina's father escorts her down the aisle first and places her hand in Daniel's. Then Samuel escorts Veronica down the aisle, her parents had died in a car accident a few years ago so she had no family left. She was so thrilled when Samuel offered to escort her down the aisle. They reach Dempie, his father then places her hand in his and the ceremony began. Our good friend Astor had become the head council member after the traitor John was destroyed so he will be preforming the marriages. After the kids said their wedding vow to each other Astor pronounced them married. After all of the congratulations were said we retired to the great hall for the banquet, I was so happy for them all! It was to learn later that Dempie and Veronica would take the throne in a few years, as I had said prior in my diary I knew he would become king some day! Daniel and Sabrina will be returning to her country since her father has no male heir Daniel will be crowned king and they will reign together. Hopefully some day soon I will become a great great grandmother, my how time flies when you are having fun! In the great hall Camaz calls the party to order and toasts to the new couples happiness. He says, "I hope that you all enjoy the happiness and joy that I have experienced with my beautiful wife all of these years. From the first day I laid eyes on her she stole my heart and I have never looked back!" Everyone then raised their glasses and toasted the happy couples. As the music began to play Camaz reached for me and took me out on the dance floor. As we slowly danced around the room I rested my head on his chest and said, "My darling that was the most beautiful thing I have ever heard you say! I love you so much, you make me so very happy!" He raises my face and bends to kiss me. "I meant everything I said my dear you are my love, my life, my everything I am nothing with out you!" Oh my, this man makes my heart sing! I pull at him and say, "Come my king let us get ready for the hunt." We go back down to our chambers and get dressed for the hunt. We have had the most delicious men and women brought in from all over for the country for the feast, they are going to be released into the jungle for us to hunt, I can hardly wait I just love the chase! A few hours later we are deep within the jungle, I have picked up on a scent and we are following it. My throat is burning wildly, there are two of them, I point up to the trees and we leap up and land on a high branch. Down below we spot the men, they are trying to cross the river. I smile at Camaz saying, "Dinner time!" I swoop down landing on one of the men, he screams out and begins to fight me. Camaz has grounded the other man and is making a quick meal of him. Now the blood lust has taken control of me, I slam the man's head to the side and strike. His wonderfully evil blood begins to flow down my throat quenching my blistering fire. I quickly drain him dry and stand up taking my loving husband's hand saying, "That was quite lovely but shall we head back to the castle? I have another hunger inside of me and only you can quench that fire!" He quickly pulls me up into his arms and leaps into the air carrying me back to the castle. A few hours later I roll off of him panting wildly. I lay there for a few minutes then fall off to sleep in my loving husbands arms.

CHAPTER 3

SAD NEWS FROM HOME

It has been several months since the wedding. I was reading the news from back home when I came across some very disturbing news. My youngest bother had been murdered, evidently he had been coming home from work, stopped to help someone that was broke down and was murdered right there along side of the road. According to the story the police had no leads into who had commented this crime. I spoke with Camaz later and told him I wanted to go back home and search for my brother's killer. This person was going to pay dearly for what he had done! We arrived at the Philadelphia airport the following evening and went to get our rental car. As I am driving to Bridgeton Camaz asks me, "Where shall we start the search for his killer?" "I was thinking about going to where he was killed and start the search from there, hopefully we can pick up his trail." I am so sad, I cannot even go to my brother's funeral or burial as the family thinks I am long dead. But I plan on finding his killer then I will bring him to the graveyard killing him at my brother's grave! We arrive in town around 3 a.m. I drive straight to where his body was found. We get out of the car then begin to test the air I quickly pick up my bother's scent. I follow it to the exact site that he was murdered, as I stand there looking down at the spot tears begin to fall down my face. Camaz comes up to me, takes me in his arms and tries to comfort me. The anger is beginning to build inside of me, I step away from him, close my eyes and let my sense of smell take over. Soon I catch it! I look at Camaz and say,"I got it! Let's go!" We begin to follow the scent, it is calling to me, I have never wanted a human's blood more than I do now! We arrive at the corner of Broad St and Cohansey St. I test the air again and can tell the smell is coming from down on Broad Street. We arrive at a rundown house. I signal for Camaz to go around the back. I then position myself at the front. I listen to see if anyone is up. He is the only one in the house and I can hear him snoring in an upstairs bedroom. I can tell there are two dogs inside of the house, but they are of no concern to me, we have the power of control over all creatures. I go up to a window on the porch, test it to see if it is unlocked, it slides up easily, I slip inside Suddenly I hear a noise I am then confronted by the dogs. I stare at them, they come up to me and begin to lick my hand. I leave them downstairs and head up to the bedroom where the man is sleeping. I quietly push open the door and walk in. He is there on the bed, I can tell that the sheets have not been washed in ages. The whole room reeks of him! My killing instinct has now kicked in, but I must control myself, I will not kill him here. I hear Camaz enter the room, I point to the man and say, "Take him and follow me to the graveyard." He picks the man up, he awakes and shouts, "What the hell, put me down!" I laugh and say, "He will put you down when I am ready to take your life for taking that of my brother!" We both leap from the window and fly off in the direction of the graveyard. I can smell my brother's scent and have no trouble finding the grave site. We land in front of the freshly dug grave, Camaz places the man on my brother's grave. I walk up to him smile, baring my fangs for him to see, saying, "For taking the life of my brother I condemn you to death by my hand." I leap on knocking him into my brother's gravestone. I hear his skull rack up against the stone. He drops to the ground and lies there bleeding from his head wound, I then slam his head to the side, strike draining him dry. We leave his body lay right there to be found the next day, I have left a note stating that I have returned from the rave to avenge my brother's death and that this is his killer, I sign the note A. I know that no one will believe that I had come back from the grave to avenge my brother's death but all that mattered to me is I know. We quickly head back to the airport board our plane and head home. While we lie in our bed awaiting the sleep of death he asks me, "Are you alright my dear? You seem lost in thought." "Yes I am fine, I was just thinking about

Our childhood growing up, I loved my brother so much!" He then

pulls me to him cradling me to his chest, I fall asleep in my

loving husbands arms.

## CHAPTER 4

## OUR RETURN HOME

We awoke to the feel of the plane touching down that evening. It is a little after 1 a.m. so we disembark the plane and head for home. We take a shower and get cleaned up before the hunt. A few hours later we are stalking the dark streets in search of prey. Camaz had picked up on a scent earlier and we are now following it. We arrive at a small house in the heart of the city. The smell of evil is all around this house. We can tell there are at least 2 men inside but no innocents. We listen to the conversation the two men are having, they are planning on robbing a bank in the morning They plan on killing everyone there so there are no witnesses but they will never make it to that bank! We go through a window in the back of the house and head for the room the men are in. I walk in first and say, "Why, hi there boys, how about a game of hide and seek?" They look at me startled then one of the men asks,

"How in the hell did you get into my house and who are you?" I smile at him saying, "I am the thing from your worst nightmares here to deliver your punishment!" I leap on the man knocking him to the ground. Just then Camaz appears in the room and quickly goes after the other man, I can hear the man screaming for his life but I am to busy dining on my prey to look up. Once we have both men drained we leave the house and head home. We arrive just before daybreak say our good nights to our family and head to our quarters. Once we are behind closed doors Camaz comes up to me and begins to undress me. He kisses me on my neck knowing how that drives me crazy with passion! I turn around then take him in my arms kissing him madly. I break our kiss then breathlessly ask, "My king would you like to join me in the shower?" He smiles at me saying, "With pleasure my queen. Lead the way." We started in the shower and ended in our bed panting loudly I roll to my side staring into those beautiful eyes and say, "If I wasn't already dead you would be the death of me some day!" He laughs at what I have said and answers, "But my one true love, I have so much more to give!" He pulls me to him kissing me passionately. A few hours later I am asleep in his arms with a smile on my face. He following evening when we arose and dressed we went upstairs to talk to Mikel and Iris. They had just returned from Paris. I had so many questions for Iris and was excited to see what she had brought back with her. We went off to a corner of the living room and begin our discussion. Soon we are laughing and having a good old time. Camaz and Mikel approach us and asks what we are laughing about. I tell them about how we both just loved the Parisian food, but we also loved the shopping. They both bust out laughing and Camaz says, "Women! All they can think about is food and shopping!" I smile up at him and say, "My king, what else is there to think about?!" He reaches for me and says, "Let's hunt!" Mikel and Iris joined us in the hunt that night, it has been awhile since they have hunted with us and I am enjoying their company. We come upon a small village right outside of our home, I have picked up something wonderfully evil. They all follow behind me as I let my sense of smell lead the way We come upon a small house on a dimly lit street. We can hear five men inside talking. We can also smell the sweet blood of innocents. Iris and I have decided to keep the men busy while our men rescue the women upstairs. There are four women in all and they are caged like animals. This makes my blood boil in anger! These men are going to pay dearly for what they have done to these women! Iris and I set our plan in motion. We go up to the front door and knock. Soon a tall thin man answers the door. We tell him that our car has broken down and that we need help. He invites us into the house. We go in looking around. We spot the other four in the dining room. The man that answered the door tells the other men that our car has broken down and that we need their help. He then winks at them, I quickly pick up on this and think to myself, oh goodie, let the games begin! One of the men tells us that his friend has a tow truck and he is going to get it. We know better but we say thank you anyway. The mans sitting at the table says, "My you are both very beautiful! To bad you will not be leaving here!" He then umps up grabs me, one of the other men has grab Iris from behind and is holding a knife at her throat. The man that has grabbed me says, "You will do what I say or my friend will slit her throat!" So I play along with his game. I so loved this game! They take us both upstairs where they are holding the other women, but we already know our men have gotten them out of the house and are lying in wait for these men. As soon as we enter the room they notice that the other women are gone. The man that is holding me asks the others, "Where the hell are they!" Just then Camaz and Mikel comes from out of he shadows. The men are startled by this and release us, they draw their weapons and ready themselves for the attack. I begin to laugh. The man turns to me and asks, "What is so funny?" I stop laughing long enough to says, "Well, lets see, you try to capture us then turn into the chickens you are when you see our men. I think that is hilarious!" The man then says, "We are not afraid of any of you!" I smile at the man baring my fangs for him to see and say, "You should be, for you see, we are death come to pay you back for everything you have done to those women!" The man then raises his gun at me and fires. I take a bullet right in the chest but it does not have any effect, it is not silver. He looks on in astonishment and says, "What the hell are you? That bullet should have killed you!" I laugh and say, "I am the creature in your nightmares come to life, for you see I am vampire!" "Please don't kill me, I promise I will never hurt another woman the rest of my life!" I stare him in the eye and say, "Sorry, to late!" I slam his head to the side and strike. His blood was so sweet with evil that I felt like I was drunk! I look over at the rest of my family they have the other men down draining them dry. Once I have finished draining my prey I just sit there for a minute. I tell Camaz, "I feel drunk, his blood was so evil!" Camaz laughs then pulls me up into his arms saying, "Then we need to get you home so that I can sober you up!" He then carries me home in his arms. A few hours later as we await our deep sleep I ask, "What happened to me? I have never been so intoxicated before!" He laughs saying, "Once in a great while we will come across a human that is so evil that his blood is like a drug to us! It sets our blood on fire and we become very intoxicated.!" I look lovingly into his eyes and say, " I hope this does not lead to me becoming an alcoholic! Do vampires have AA?" Camaz burst out laughing and says, "You never cease to amaze me my queen!" I then fall of to sleep with a smile on my face.

CHAPTER 5

THE GREAT UPRISING

A few months later we where returning to the castle after our hunt when we came upon a wounded vampire. His name is Sampson he tells us that he was attacked by werewolves. We take him back to the castle and to the healers. The following evening when we arose we went up to see how our guest was doing. He was sitting in the living room reading one of my books. Camaz then says to him, "Well my friend, you are looking much better." He smiles at us and says, "I am much better. Thank you for helping me!" He tells us that he has traveled here from Spain and has come to ask the king and queen for help. Just then Samuel and Kim entered the room. We introduce Sampson to them and he begins to tell us why he has come asking for help. "Sires a great uprising is happening in our country, we have become overrun with werewolves! Their leader is viscous and deadly! He has capture our queen and is going to kill her. Our king, Manuel, has heard of your great battles and has sent me to request your assistance with trying to get our queen back. I think to myself, "Oh no, here we go again! Will this never end! Samuel speaks, "We understand your plight but we must first discuss this issue with our council. If you will excuse us we will go and speak with them." We all leave the room and head to the council's chambers. While we are walking Camaz ask, "What do you think my dear, should we help them?" I think for a moment, I can still remember the werewolf's claws ripping my back open. I answer, "I would not want her to suffer the way I have in the past from werewolves. So I say we help!" He smiles at me saying, "My queen, you have a good and true heart! That is why I love you so!!" We arrive at the council's chambers and discuss the problem, they all agree that we should help the king of Spain, but Samuel and Kim need to stay behind. They are not happy with this but they agree to stay here. We leave the council's chambers and head back to where Sampson is. We give him the news and he is quite pleased. We tell him that we need to go to the headquarters of our vampire elite to have them make ready for our trip. A few hours later we are in the town of Cristos. Where our elite squad is headquartered. Our great fairy warrior Dempie's son has joined the elite squad and is as mighty a warrior as his father was. He looks so much like his father it is eerie! All of our warriors have gathered in the great war room. We Introduce them all to Sampson and get down to business. We make our plans to leave and rescue the queen. Our plane leaves the following evening for Spain. I have picked up the second book in the series about the young girl that has fell in love with a vampire. Wow can this woman write! As I felt the plane begin to descent I put up my book and got ready for battle. I have placed my sword in its sheath behind my back and my daggers are on both arms. I have chosen a leather outfit that is skin tight. As I pull my hair back into a ponytail Camaz comes up tome, takes me in his arms and says, "My god, you look so sexy in that outfit, shall I take it off?" I laugh at what he has said and reply, "Now you know that we have no time for fun and games! We have a queen to rescue!" He kisses me, I whisper into his mouth, "I promise, you may undress me to your hearts desire later my love!" We then depart the plane. There are several vans there awaiting our arrival. We all load up and head to the palace to speak with King Manuel. Once we arrive and all of the introductions are made we sit down to discuss the rescue of the queen. We learn that her name is Isabella and they have ruled this country for centuries. They have no children as she was a human before becoming vampire. I felt very sad that they have never had the joy of children, if we bring her back here safely, and if they are interested, we will tell them how it is possible. Just then another vampire enters the room and tells the king they have just received intel on where the queen is being held. So we all loaded up in the vans and headed to where she is being held. We arrive at the location about an hour later. The smell of werewolf is heavy in this area! So strong that it is causing me flashbacks to my attacks. Camaz can see the distress in my face, he takes my hand and says, "Are you alright my dear? You look frightened." I look up at him and say, "I will be okay, it's just that the scent of werewolf is so strong that it is bringing back memories of my attacks!" He takes me in his arms saying, "It will be okay my queen, I will be at your side the whole time I promise!' He kisses me gently. We all were given something belonging to the queen so that we could scent her. I close my eyes and let my sense of smell take over, testing the air for her. All of a sudden I pick up her scent. I look to the others and say, "There, in that small house at the foot of the mountain, that is where they are holding her, she is still alive." We begin to descend down to the house. Just before we reach the house we are rushed by hundreds of werewolves. Camaz pushes me behind him and makes ready for battle. I draw my sword from my back and ready myself for the attack. He quickly takes the heads of the first two that charge us. My keen hearing picks up on the sound of one behind me, I swing around to face my attacker. He is huge, over seven feet tall! He reminds me of the monster werewolf that almost killed me years ago. He charges me. I drop to the ground making him miss. I then leap to my feet, come around with my blade and catch him across the chest. He roars out in pain then swings his huge claws at me. I think to myself, oh shit here we go again! I drop again causing the massive paw to miss me. I leap straight up into the air. I then come back down with a vengeance. I swing my sword at his head severing it from his body. His head drops to the ground followed by his massive body. I look for Camaz and find him in battle with three of them. He is moving so fast that it is hard to see him. Within growl, "Stop, if you come any close I will kill her!"He has his massive paw, with all of those razor sharp claws, at her throat. I am afraid of this werewolf but I must try and stop him. I say to him, "Why have you taken this woman? She has done nothing to you!" He laughs and says, "And just who are you my pretty little vampire?" "I am the former queen of Mexico and this is my king. We have come to rescue Isabella." He says, "I have heard many tales if your husband and you, you are the little vampire that took my brother's life! I will make you a deal. I will release her if you come take her place." Camaz yells at the beast, "Never! I will not let you have her! Come beast and let us do battle!" I can still remember what this creature's brother did to Camaz and I will not let that happen again. I charge the beast with my sword draw. I begin to circle him and say, "Come then beast, let's dance!" The beast charges me knocking me to the ground but before I can get back up Camaz is on the beast. He has driven his dagger deep into the beast chest. He screams out in pain and slings Camaz off of him. The other two werewolves in the room have now come after me. The black one rushes me with his claws fully extended, ripping my arm. I scream, drop to the ground, roll and come back up swinging, I take his head in one swing. The second one is in such shock at what I have done he is momentary distracted. I draw both of my daggers from my wrist braces and run at him full

force. Strike and drive them deep into his chest. He screams out in

pain, I can see his flesh start to burn from the silver blades. He

backs away form me clutching his chest. I run to where my sword

is, grab it and run at the beast swinging. I catch him in the neck

removing his head. I turn to look for Camaz. The white werewolf

is on him and is readying for the final blow. I scream out, "No!" I

run toward the beast with my sword. He raises his massive paw

and readies to remove Camaz's head. I land on the beast's back

and knock him off of Camaz. He has cut him deep with his claws

across his chest and he is losing blood. My vision becomes

blurred with red, the hatred is building within me. I turn to the

beast with my eyes blazing red. I watch as the the fear enters his

face. I run at him again, leap and land square in his chest. I raise

my sword and with one quick swing remove his head. I fall off of

the beast and just lay there. I look over at Camaz he smiles and

says, "I am beginning to get use to the red eyes!" I smile at him and say, " Aren't we a pair. Always getting ourselves ripped up by some creature!" My arm is beginning to hurt really bad, the pain is intense! I quickly get up, go over to my beloved reach my hand to him and help him up. He has many deep claw marks all over his body. We both need to get back to the castle. We go into the next room and find Isabella. We untie her and leave this terrible place. We arrive at the castle about an hour later. King Maunel has taken us to his healers, Camaz's wounds are much worse than mine and will take longer for him to heal. I take him to our quarters and begin the blood transfer that will aid in his healing. I have ask for our food to be brought in for a few days as I need my strength to heal Camaz. Once I have finished feeding I offer my neck to him, he bites down gently and begins to drink. After a few days he is looking much better, all of his wounds are healing nicely and the wound in my arm is completely gone. I offer him my neck one more time but he says, "No. I no longer need your blood, I crave your body!" He then takes me in his arms and kisses me. I can feel the fire building way down low. I grunt, he says, "Oh I know that sound. Are you ready for me?" "Oh yes my king, I am so ready for you!" He rolls me over looking deep into my eyes. I feel as though he is looking into my soul and likes what he sees. He says, "My queen, you are the most beautiful creature to ever have been placed on this earth! I love you with my heart and soul!" I smile at him and say, "As I love you!" He gently lowers himself and enters me. I scream out his name with each orgasm. A few hours later I fall off to sleep in his arms. The next evening we say goodbye to our new friends and head back home.

# CHAPTER 6

## A SURPRISE FOR CAMAZ

We have been back home now for six months. I have been doing a lot of thinking and have decided on something. While we are out hunting I tell Camaz I have something I want to discuss with him. He takes me in his arms and asks, "What does my queen desire?" "I have been thing about this for awhile and I want to have another child!" He looks at me in astonishment then replies, "Are you sure? Can you handle that again after what Katrina did to us?" I think about that for a minute then reply, "Yes my love. I have been wanting another child for a long time." "Then we shall give you another! Whatever my queen's heart desires!" He wrapped his arms around me hugging me to his chest. I look up at him with tears of joy in my eyes and say, "I love you!" I told Camaz that I wanted to chose the surrogate this time. After what happened with Katrina I wasn't taking any chances. So our invitations were sent out to all eligible royals around the world. In a few weeks we had received replies back from them. I made a list and invited them to our home. I would be the one interviewing them. We planned a great ball in their honor. While the party was going on I watched each of them carefully to see if any interest in Camaz was present. Then one by one I look them off and talked to them. By the end of the evening I have chosen three possibilities, Princess Carmen from Spain, princess Sophia from Romania and Princess Celeste from England. I have ask the three princesses to stay a few weeks so Camaz and I could come to know them better. The others returned to their homes the next evening. Over the next two weeks I got to know the ladies very well, but I had come to like Sophia the best. We had become great friends So while we are laying in bed waiting for sleep to take us I say to Camaz, "My darling, I have made my decision. I would like Sophia to carry our child." He smiles at me and says, "As you wish my queen." So we said farewell to the other ladies and began make the preparations for the conception. Three days later Camaz went off with Sophia to conceive our third child. The next evening they returned and said that all had gone well. So now we wait, I am so excited to be having a baby again. We had lost our second child at birth, something had gone terribly wrong and she did not make it, I have mourned her lost for fifteen years now. We lost her and the surrogate that day. Camaz told me later that sometimes that happens but it is very rare. It has been three weeks since the conception and we are making ready for the arrival of our new child. Sophia is on the third floor where all of the children have been birthed. I have been spending a lot of time with her and we have become the best of friends. She has told me the story of how she had found her human lover and that she planned to marry him soon. I told her how happy I was for her then I ask her if she would like to have the wedding here. She thanked me for the offer but declined stating that her father had already begun the plans at home. In the middle of the fourth week we received word that she had delivered a little girl and has requested our presence upstairs. I grab Camaz's hand and pull him toward the staircase. I say, "Come my love, let us go look upon our new child." We knock on the door and she asks us to come in. We walk over to the bed and there in her arms was the most beautiful little girl I have ever laid eyes on. I ask, "May I hold her?" "Yes my dear friend, she is your daughter!" I pick the child up and stare into the most beautiful blue eyes I have ever seen! I said, "Wow look at her eyes, they are blue like mine! I had expected them to be emerald green as yours my husband." We took our new daughter down to the nursery next to our quarters, and placed her in the crib. I turn to Camaz and say, "I still cannot believe her blue eyes!" He takes me into his arms and says, "My queen that is because she is also part of you!" I ask, "How is that possible?" "Each time we have shared blood a little of you is passed on to me and me to you." I think about that for a minute then say, "Wow, so she got her eye color from me? That means that she has my genes as well! Oh husband, I am so happy that I am a part of our child as well!" He kisses me gently and says, "Yes and she will be as beautiful as her mother!" I am so happy, this is the best news he could have ever told me. A few days later Sophia left for home. We have been invited to her wedding and will be attending in a the near future. I watch as Camaz plays with the baby on our bed. Camaz asks, "Has my queen decided on a name for our little princess?" I look at him lovingly and respond, "Yes, her name shall be Makla. What do you think?" He smiles and says, "I love it! We will take her to the council tomorrow evening and present her to them." I coddle her close to my chest and tell her how much her mommy loves her. It has been three months since Makla's birth and I am ready to go out and hunt. Kim wants to watch the baby while we are gone so I know she is in good hands, Kim would guard her with her life. We leave the castle for the hunt. I have told Camaz that I feel like running. It has been awhile since I have felt the wind in my face. He says,

"Then come my queen let us run!" He takes off in a sprint with me close on his heels, I have grown faster over the years and I am almost as fast as him. We are high up in the mountains now searching for prey. We leap off of a cliff and land on the other side. I have picked up on a smell that I must have. My throat is burning wildly with desire. I point to the east and take off running again, Camaz is right beside of me. We come upon a clearing and stop, testing the air for our dinner. I can hear his strong heartbeat a few feet away. His blood is calling to me. I pick up on another scent just as strong. I look at Camaz and smile, saying, "Oh goodie, there are two of them!" He smiles at me then we drop down into our hunting crouch and begin to stalk them. We come up on a campsite where the two men are staying. The pull of their blood is so strong it takes everything in me to restrain myself. For you see, they also have an innocent in their campsite. A young woman they have tied up in the tent. They have taken turns raping her and she is very weak. I look at Camaz and signal him to go around the back of the tent to save the girl. The hatred in me is building and they are going to pay for what they have done to this poor innocent girl! Both men are at the campfire cooking their dinner. I walk out from behind the tree I was standing at and say, "Hello boys, my name is Anne and I have come for some fun! Who wants to party with me?" They both smile at me then the taller of the two says, "Beautiful I would love to party with you!" I walk up to him stare him in the eyes and say, "Okay big boy go into the woods, I do not want your friend watching." He smiles then takes my hand, turns to his friend and says, "Catch you later." Then we leave. Camaz has alerted me that he has freed the woman and is going after the other man. I tell him to enjoy his meal. I lead the man to an open field, remove my clothes and lie down on the soft grass. He stares down at me then says, "My god, you are so beautiful! I cannot believe you have gotten naked for me!" I smile up at him baring my fangs and say, "Why silly man I have not gotten naked for you, I am naked for my husband.!" I then spring up and knock him to the ground slam his head to the side and strike draining him dry. I roll off his body and stare up at the night sky. The stars are shining bright. A few minutes later Camaz approaches me, looks down and says, "My god woman, you are positively glowing in the moonlight!" I smile up at him and say, "Come my king I have a fire way down low that I need you to put out!" I watch as he removes his clothes, I still marvel at his beautiful body. His manhood would make any man envious, alive or UN-dead! He hovers over my body, I stare into his beautiful green eyes. I tell him how much I love him. We make love under the stars for hours, then lie in each others arms and stare at the beautiful night sky. I roll over and say, "Are you ready to go home my king? I miss Makla." He smiles at me and says, "Then lets go home my queen, I am ready to see our beautiful daughter as well." We race home and up the stairs to look upon our daughter. She is awake and cooing at us. I pick her up from her crib and hold her close to my heart. I kiss her on top her head and tell her how much her mommy and daddy love her. She looks up at me with those beautiful blue eyes and smiles. Her tiny fangs glistening in the light. She is old enough now to drink from a living host so we take her down to the holding cells. I pick one of the most evil men here and enter his cell carrying Makla. She is a natural, she catches him with her eyes and he becomes limp, I place her at his throat and she begins to feed.

CHAPTER 7

MAKLA'S FIRST BIRTHDAY

Today is Makla's first birthday she has grown into a beautiful child. She looks to be about six in human years. Camaz has told me that she looks more and more like me every day! She has long brown hair the color of mine and those beautiful blue eyes. She has also become quite a skilled huntress! She loves the chase. We have hunted as a family since she had taken her first steps. We have planned a birthday party for her. We have invited all royals with children of her age. My best friends, Louisa and Marylou will be attending as they had their children around the same time we had Makla. I am so excited to see them both and the children for I have not seen either of them yet. Louisa's little boy is named Louis and Marylou's little girl is named Anne after me. I was so proud when she told me that she had named her daughter after me. A few days later everyone had arrived, the children where absolutely adorable! We have made ready all of the rooms I hug my two best friends and take them upstairs to their rooms. We have made up the adjourning rooms for the children. The children are all off playing in Makla's room. This gives me time to catch up with my friends. Louisa tells me that she and Richard are planning on having another child as soon as Louis comes of age. She asks me if Camaz and I are planning on having anymore. I tell her I don't think so but we will see. We all bust out laughing. Just then all of our husbands walk into the room Camaz asks, "What are my three favorite ladies laughing about?" I smile at him and say, "Nothing, just a private joke." He says, "Well then, are you ladies ready for dinner?" I look at my loving husband and say, "Yes we are starving!" I tell him that I have longed for a good chase. So we go down to the cells and pick a prey of each of us. We then take them out to the woods and release them. I say, "Oh goodie, food on the run!" We give them a fifteen minute start and then take to the air. They have all taken off in different directions. So we pick our dinner by scent and go after them. I have chosen a very yummy smelling man. His whole body reeks of evil and sets my throat to burning. I spot him below in an open field,. He has stopped to catch his breath. I see him panting wildly. I swoop down on him like a large bird of prey and carry him into the air. He is now screaming at the top of his lungs, yelling for me to put him down, I laugh at that and say, "But my dear man, if I do that then I will be spoiling my dinner!" He looks up at me and I smile showing him my fangs. Now he is really screaming, I can see on his face that he knows what I am. He begins to plead for his life, telling me that he has a wife and children. I laugh and say, "You should have thought of them before you started killing people!" I then land on the ground with him on his back, I push his head to the side and drink him in deeply. His sweet evil blood quinces the blistering fire in my throat. I stand up from the man and wipe the blood from my mouth and then lick my fingers. My, my, was he delicious! A few minutes later I hear Camaz calling to me in my head I let him know where I am at. He tells me he will be at my side in a few minutes. While I am waiting for my one true love, I stare up at the beautiful night sky. God, how I loved the night! We all arrive back at the castle and check on the children. They have all feed and are ready for their long sleep. I tuck Makla in and tell her how much I love her. She kisses me on my cheek and says, "I love you to Momma!" We tell her "Sweet dreams!" then Camaz kisses her goodnight. We then head for our bedroom. Once in our room, he takes me in his arms and says, "Do you know how happy you make me, my beautiful queen?" I look at him lovingly and say, "I'm not sure, do you think you can show me?" He laughs and says, "Come here!" He then pulls me to his lips and shows me, for hours, just how much he loves me! The following evening the party was a great success The children had a blast. We even released their dinner into the woods so that they could hunt. Of course we were close by to make sure nothing happened to them. I watched as Makla took down her prey, she reminds me so much of her father! She looks up from the body and smiles at me, it just amazes me that with each month she looks more and more like me! The following evening we said our goodbyes to our friends. Makla is very sad, she has grown to love her two new friends and will miss them so much. We promise the children that they will be together next year for her second birthday.

# CHAPTER 8

## MAKLA'S SECOND BIRTHDAY

Well the day had finally arrived for Makla's second birthday. She has grown into a stunning pre-teen. She is almost as tall as me and her long brown hair flows down her back in ringlets. She is so excited to see her friends Louis and Anne, they have kept in contact by the internet. Facebook is a strange and wonderful way of communication over great distances and I am fascinated with Skype, I can actually see my best friends when talking to them. Oh this modern world, what will they think of next? After the party tonight will be the first official hunt for the children by themselves. We are allowing them to go into the city hunting. Of course we will be close by if they need us, but they must learn to hunt on their own. I watch as Makla sits atop a building and test the air for her prey. I see her catch the smell and leap to the ground below. She begins to come up behind a man on the street corner. She looks up at him with those beautiful blue eyes and says, "Mister, can you help me, I am lost?" I can tell from his scent that he is a child molester and killer. The man tells her that he lives right around the corner and will take her to his house so he can call the police. She smiles up at him but does not show her fangs and says, "Thank you mister, you are very kind." Boy, my girl is good! She goes inside the house with the man a few minutes later I hear him start to scream. She then comes out takes to the sky and heads for home. I go into the house just to make sure that the man is dead. His body is growing cold so I leave and head for home. I pickup on Camaz's scent, he is in the middle of the hunt. I sit atop a building and watch as he stalks his prey. God ,I love to watch him hunt! Then I pick up on a most delectable scent that I must have. I am soon stalking the dark streets looking for my next meal. I reach my target within minutes. The man is standing on a corner smoking a cigarette. I watch as he snubs it out under his foot. I begin walking toward the man. He senses my presences. Turns and says, "Why hello there pretty lady, it is kind of late for you to be out, someone might just try and get you!" I smile at the man baring my fangs and say, "Oh I just came out for a midnight snack." I then leap on him knocking him to the ground. I sink my fangs deep within the softness of his neck and enjoy my stack. Good to the last drop! All of a sudden I hear a laugh from behind me. I jump up turn and see a strange vampire I have never met before. I have not brought my weapons with me so I almost defenseless. He walks towards me and says, "Hello there little vampire, my name is Tomas. And what may I ask, is your name?" Now I'm pissed I hate being called little vampire and my blood begins to boil. I look at him and say, "What do you want? Can't you see that I am busy with my meal!" He answers, "Well I thought that we could get together. You are very beautiful and an expert huntress. Just what I have been looking for!" I look at him odd and say, "Sorry but I am already spoken for." I then begin to leave. He grabs my arm and says, "Where are you going little one? I have not finish with you yet!" Now I am really pissed, I turn to him with my eyes blazing red and say, "Let go of my arm if you want to stay alive!" He looks at my eyes, and asks, "What is wrong with your beautiful blue eyes? They are now bright red!" Then I hear my beloved's voice. "That is because you have called her little vampire, she hates that with a passion. I suggest you release my wife's arm before she rips you a new one!" The man quickly releases me, turns to Camaz and says, "You are a very lucky man to have such a beautiful and gifted wife! I will bother her no more!" He then leaps into the air and flies off. I run and jump into Camaz's arms. I then tell him, "I am so glad you were near by and heard my call! I was so afraid he was going to take me! I could not bare to go though that again, I would have killed myself first!" He kisses me ever so gently then says, "I told you I would never let anything like that happen to you again and I meant it!" He then leaps into the air carrying me back to our home. The following evening we said goodbye to all of our friends and told

them that we would see them next year for Makla's coming of age

party.

# CHAPTER 9

## MAKLA'S COMING OF AGE

It has now been three years since Makla's birth and she has grown into a fine young woman. Sometimes when I look at her it is like looking into a mirror! We have planned her coming of age party and it is set for tomorrow night. But before the party she will stand before the council and be proclaimed an adult. She has told us that she wants to go away to college for a few years. I am sad at her leaving but she is an adult now and I must let her go. It is around 9 p.m. when everyone begins to arrive. My best friends have arrived first and we are upstairs catching up on everything. The children are out in the courtyard enjoying the summer evening. Louis has grown into a striking young man. He has his father's rugged good looks and his mother's beautiful green eyes. Marylou's daughter has grown into an extraordinary beauty, she has jet black hair and jade colored eyes. She is small framed like her mother. After the ceremony and party we all take to the woods to hunt. Several hours later we return home all with full bellies. We say goodnight to our friends and family and head for our quarters. Makla is already in her room and is listening to music. We both kiss her goodnight and tell her how much we love her. Once we are in our room I close the door behind us, Camaz takes me in his arms and kisses me. He breaks our kiss then says, "What is bothering you my dear, you seam distracted?" I look at him and say, "I don't now, I just have this terrible feeling that something bad is going to happen!" "Love nothing is going to happen." I reach up and kiss him and say, "I'm sure you are right but I just cannot seem to shake this feeling of dread!" As the sun rises I fall of to sleep with this weighing very heavy on my mind. For the second time in my UN-dead life I dream. In the dream I am being chased by the rapist vampire that took me and I cannot get away from him. I am screaming Camaz's name over and over but he does not hear me. I suddenly shoot straight up in our bed screaming Camaz takes me in his arms and tries to calm me. Blood tears are streaking down my face. He looks me in the eyes and asks, "Are you alright my dear? You woke up screaming my name!" "Oh Camaz, I was being chased by the rapist vampire and I couldn't get away from him. I kept calling your name but you could not hear me!" He hugs me to his chest saying, "There, there my dear, it was only a dream. He cannot harm you, he is dead!" "I know but it was just so vivid!" He pulls me to his lips and kisses me tenderly then says, "I will die before that will ever happen to you again!" I fall back to sleep in his arms and the rest of my sleep was dreamless. The following evening when I awoke I still had that feeling of dread. I get up, dress myself and go to our daughter's room to see if she would like to go hunting with us. But she is not there. I let Camaz know I am going upstairs to find her and he lets me know he will be up soon. I go up to the living room but she is not there. I begin to search the castle. I am getting frantic now, I cannot find her anywhere. Just then Camaz comes into the room, he can see the fear on my face, he asks, "What is wrong?" I reply, "I cannot find Makla anywhere. I have searched the entire castle, she is not here." He says, "Maybe she was hungry and has left for the hunt already."No she has never left without telling us before even, if she is going hunting! I know something is wrong!" We go outside of the castle and begin to test the air for her scent. I soon pick it up and take off running Camaz is right behind me. Then I stop dead in my tracks and test the air again. There is another scent, it is a vampire! I immediately know who's it is! I turn to Camaz and say, "Oh no, it is the vampire we met on the night of her two year party! He has taken my baby, we must hurry!" I can see the anger building in Camaz's eyes as he says, "If he has done anything to our daughter. I will rip him to pieces!" We come to an area where both of their scents are very strong. I let my ears range out to see if I can pick up on our daughter. Then all of a sudden I hear her! She is fighting this vampire trying to get him off of her. We reach the opening of a cave and run inside, we both have our swords drawn. We come out into an open area and spot them. He has her pinned down on the ground and is trying to rape her. I scream at him to get away from my daughter. He looks up in disbelief and says, "Daughter, I thought it was you. You two could pass for twins! I wish your daughter no harm it is you that I want!" Camaz screams at him, "Never!" He then rushes the vampire, but he has put a sword to our daughter's neck and says, "Stop or I will destroy her!" Camaz stops in his tracks and says, "Please release our child she means nothing to you but everything to us!" He smiles at Camaz and says, "If she means so much to you both then have your wife come to me of her own free will!" I start to walk toward him but Camaz stops me and says, "No you cannot do this. You do not understand what he is asking of you. If you go to him of your own free will it will break our bond and you will be his!" I look into his eyes and say, "You are my one true love and soul mate, I will love you for all of eternity but I cannot allow harm to come to our daughter!" I say to the vampire, "I agree to your terms. Now release my daughter!" At that moment I felt something snap within me. I felt all alone as if Camaz had left me. I look at him and say, "Why do I feel so alone? I feel as if you have left me and my heart is being ripped from my chest!" "By agreeing with his terms you have broken our blood bond. You are now free of my will." I begin to cry, the blood tears rolling down my face. I go over to where the man is and he releases our daughter. She runs up to me and says, "Oh mother, I am so sorry! I would have gladly given my life not to see you in so much pain! I know how much you love father and what this evil man has done to you!" She hugs me fiercely to her. I release her and say, "It is alright my daughter, you are safe, that is all that matters to me! Now go to your father and get out of this terrible place!" Camaz looks at the man and says, "Some day I will come for her and take back what is mine! You may have her, now, but I promise it will not be for long!" He leaves the cave with Makla. The man looks at me and says, "Remember you have done this of your own free will. I will be taking you back to my home to complete our blood bond. I would do it now but I am required to present you to my council before taking you for my bride as I have taken your from another." We leave the cave. He leaps into the air with me and we leave. I am screaming out in my head for Camaz but receive no answer. The broken bond has also broken our mental bond as well. We reach a small airport, I am not sure where it is. He takes me aboard the plane. He tells his pilot to ready for takeoff. I begin to sink within myself, hoping that the darkness will claim me and take me away from all of this pain, but it does not. Little did I know that Camaz had everyone out looking for us and we where now being followed.

CHAPTER 10

I AM SO ALONE

A few hours later, I feel the plane touch down. He takes me to a waiting car. We drive for a few more hours and come upon a great palace. I am taken from the car and lead into the palace. He takes me upstairs to a large bedroom having me sit on the bed. He asks me if I am hungry. I tell him no and to leave me alone. He looks at me and says, "I will not touch you until our blood bond, then you will be mine to use in anyway I desire!" He leaves the room locking the door behind him. I sit on the bed and begin to think, "Anne you have been in worst things than this and have been able to free yourself, think girl, think!" I begin scanning the room taking in every little detail. I check the windows but there is something on them that is stopping me from opening them. I go into the bathroom and check the windows there, I have the same problem. The only thing I can think of is they have been reinforced with some kind of magic to keep a vampire in. I go back to the bed and begin to think again. I must find a way to keep Tomas off of me. Then I remember when I was bitten by the ghoul and the madness had taken me. If I could pull off faking the madness, maybe he will leave me alone. So I lie in the bed and await his return. I hear him coming so I begin my act. I start screaming to Camaz to make the monsters go away, that the ghoul has bitten me and the monsters are everywhere. Tomas comes rushing into the room after hearing my screams. I am thrashing about on the bed. I do say I am putting on a pretty good show. He looks down at me and says, "What is wrong with you woman? Have you lost your mind!" I continue to put on the show screaming Camaz's name over and over asking him to make the monsters go away. Tomas begins to shake me saying, "Snap out of it woman!" He then smacks me hard across my face. I am so stunned I look at him and say, "Why did you hit me, I have done nothing to you!" He says, "You where mad woman you where screaming that you where being chased by monsters!" I look at him and say, "Oh that, it happens all the time. I was bitten by a ghoul several years back and the madness takes me whenever it wants! I am sorry I frightened you." He says, "I have never heard of a vampire surviving the bite of a ghoul. You are just fooling me!" "I am sorry but you are wrong, I did survive the attack but now I am chased by the madness. Go ask your council, they will tell you the truth." He begins to leave the room but turns to say, "If you are lying to me I will kill you myself!" He leaves the room locking the door behind him. I sit up in the bed and smile. My plan is working! The memories of the madness are so vivid in my mind that I can create them over and over again. Boy is he in for some bad days! He returns to the room and tells me the council has confirmed what I have told him about the madness. That if a vampire does survive the madness would stay with them for all of eternity. He says, "If I had known this I would never have taken you. For you see, the council will not allow me to take a bride that is plagued with madness. I release you from your promise and you are free to go." "Go! Where would I go!! You have taken the only thing that mattered to me, my one true love. You have broken our bond and now you are responsible for me!" "That is where you are wrong, I have released you and you are free. I will have the plane made ready to take you back to Mexico." I think to myself, "Oh goodie, I can get the hell out of here!" He has one of his guards escort me to the plane to make sure I got on it. A few hours later I was back in my beloved Mexico. I left the plane and ran as fast as my legs could carry me back to the castle. When I arrived no one was there to greet me. I ran to the council's chambers to find out what was going on. Astor tells me that everyone has gone out searching for me. That Camaz said he would not rest until he brought me back home. I ask him, "Astor do you know where he has gone? I must find him to let him know I am safe!" He then proceeds to tell me Camaz had received intel on where Tomas had taken me and he was on the way there now. I say my farewells and run from the council's chambers. I take to the air. I know Tomas was the ruler of Peru, so I fly there as fast as I can. I cannot take the plane as it had already left. I know it will take me a few hours to fly but I must reach my love before daybreak! A few hours later I arrive in Peru. I scent the air for Tomas, as this will be the easiest way for me to find the castle! I catch his scent. I begin running like the wind for I have also caught Camaz's scent, that means he is here already! I reach Tomas's castle in a matter of minutes. I spot Camaz in the distance he looks like he is getting ready to storm the castle. I run at him full force and leap into his arms knocking him backward on to the ground. He looks up at me smiles and saying, "I have missed you too my queen! How did you ever get away from his hold on you?" I pull him to his feet and say, "Come we need to leave this place, I will explain everything to you once we are on our plane heading back home." We take to the air and fly back to where our plane is waiting, board it and leave this place for good.

Once in the air I tell Camaz the whole story of how I had tricked Tomas into believing the madness had taken me and once he had talked to his council, he released me from my promise. Camaz laughs and says, "Very cleaver my queen!" I begin to cry, he takes me in his arms and asks, "What is wrong dear heart?" "Oh Camaz, that evil man has broken our blood bond I feel as if I have lost you for all of eternity!" He wipes the tears from my face and says, "Do not worry yourself, my queen, we shall go down to our sleeping quarters and I shall bond you to me again!" Down below he explains what the process would entail for us to become a bonded pair again. He would have to take my blood to almost the point of death. He would then strike again but this time he would not take anything and this would leave his gene behind again. He also told me, " I am sorry, my dear, but you will be human. But I will be by your side the entire time!" He lies me down on the bed stares into my eyes and says, "The next time you open those beautiful eyes my dear we will be bonded!" He gently moves my head to one side, strikes and begins to drink. As he drinks I can feel my life leaving my body, I begin to float upward above myself, I look down at Camaz, he is still drinking from me, then suddenly I feel my heart thump alive! I cannot believe it my heart is beating!! I see him raise up from my neck and strike again leaving it just as quickly. Then I am falling, down toward my body, then I am inside, I feel all of my human senses come alive. Then the burning began, oh my did it ever. I felt like my whole body was ablaze! I begin screaming for Camaz then I hear his soothing voice in my head, I begin to concentrate on his soothing voice as I fight the blistering fire. I was so happy he was with me again, it made the burning worth every licking flame. I begin to feel the fire leave my limbs and draw into my heart. It is beating severely trying to out race the scorching fire. I feel it take it's final beat and come to a shattering halt. I lie there for a minute then open my eyes. Camaz is looking down at me with pride shining in his eyes. I leap from the bed straight into his arms and kiss him madly. I break our kiss and say, "Oh Camaz my heart sings for you, I am the happiest woman on earth! Oh how I have missed you!" He smiles at me and says, "Welcome home my beautiful queen. I am so happy to have you back with me! I can feel our bond and it is stronger than ever!" I pull him back to my lips and show him just how happy I am to be back home! A few hours later I lay in my loving husbands arms panting wildly. He raises up on his elbow and looks down at me. He says, "My one true love, you have no idea how my heart ached for you when you chose to go with him! I felt our bond break and my heart broke with it!" "I know my darling, but I had to do it for our daughter! I could not let that monster kill her!" He takes me in his arms and pulls me to his chest saying, "I will never lose you again dear heart, I will lay down my life before that happens again!" I smile up at him saying, "I know you would, my king, as I would for you!" I fell off into my deep sleep, there would be no dreams tonight, for you see my dreams have all come true!

CHAPTER 11

RETURN TO PARIS

The next evening when we awoke I told Camaz I wanted to make a trip back to Paris. We had such fun there that I wanted to return for a vacation. He took me in his arms and whispered, "Anything for my beautiful queen!" I pull at him and say, "Let's hunt, I am starving!" So off we went in search of our next meal. We arrive deep in the heart of the city, landing atop the tallest building letting our sense of smell range out for our prey. I am so happy to be by his side again and hunting! Even though I was only gone for a few days it had felt like an eternity! I suddenly catch the smell of something wonderful. My throat begins to burn wildly. Oh my this man was so evil, I could hardly wait to sink my fangs into his neck. I point to the west and leap into the sky following the wonderful smell. Camaz has also caught the scent of his prey, but he refuses to leave my side. He has told me he will not hunt until I have finished. The man I have honed in on is a street pusher selling drugs. He has an innocent with him right now so I sit atop the building and wait for the innocent to leave. As soon as the man is gone I swoop down on the drug dealer and carry him high into the air. At first he is too startled to scream, but all of a sudden he is fighting me and screaming for help. I laugh and say, "Shut up silly and stop fighting it will do you no good." I set down in a field with my prey, I am so hungry that I strike at once. His blood begins to flow, I drink him in enjoying every sweet evil drop. I hear a laugh from behind me. I turn and look up, Camaz is standing there watching me. He say, "It never ceases to amaze me at how ravenous you are my dear." I smile at him and say, "What can I say. I enjoy a good meal!" He reaches for my hand and says, "Shall we go, my dear, I still have yet to feed and I am hungry." We take to the air searching for Camaz's prey from earlier. We only have a few hours of night left and I am ready to be back in our room with his arms around me. The following evening when we arise we go up to make sure everything has been made ready for our trip to Paris. We have invited Louisa and Richard on our little vacation and they will be meeting us tomorrow evening in Paris. We have gone out for dinner before our flight and are now stalking our prey. We had received word that there had been a series of killings a few towns over so we are headed in that direction. I stop for a moment and test the air. All I can smell at the moment is the sweet blood of the innocent. My throat is burning wildly but I let my senses fan out further for the smell of evil. I soon pick up on that wonderful scent and begin to stalk my prey, there are three of them in all. Camaz is following closely behind me. We reach the area where the wonderful smell is coming from and spot the three men at a small campsite right outside of town. I test the air to see if there are innocents nearby, but I cannot pick up any. I think to myself, "Good we can get right down to business!" The three men are huddled around the campfire and planning their next attack. We both walk out of the woods and up to their campsite. One of the men looks up and says,"Can we help you with something?" I say, "Yes as a matter of fact you can We are very hungry and are looking for a meal." I smile at the man baring my fangs for him to see. He stares at me in disbelief and says, "Oh shit, vampires!" They all go for their guns but we are to fast for them. I have the man that had spoken down on the ground draining him. Camaz has another also and is draining him. The third man has taken off toward the woods. I stand up from my prey and say, "I am going after the other one." Camaz smiles at me and says, "Have fun!" I take to the air in search of the other man. It does not take me long to find him. He has hidden himself behind a fallen tree. I can smell the fear in him. His heart is beating wildly. I swoop down and land on the other side of the tree, I say, "Come out, come out where ever you are." I come around to where the man is hidden and say, "Tag your it!" The man jumps up screaming and takes off running. I take off after him, leap and knock him to the ground. He begins to fight me wildly making his heart take off like a race car. Now my killing instinct has kicked in. I slam his head to the side and strike drinking him dry. I roll off the man and look up at the night sky. My god it is so beautiful! Then I hear my sweet man's voice, "My dear you look so full! Shall I carry you home?" I look up at him and say, "You might just have to! I am so full!" He laughs, picks me up and takes to the air. We arrive back at our home a few minutes later and head for our quarters. Once inside of our room he begins to undress me and asks, "Shall I bathe you, my beautiful queen?" I smile up at him and say, "That would be quite lovely!" He picks me up into his arms and carries me into the bathroom, sits me down beside the tub, and begins to draw my bath. Our tub is quite large so he joins me in the bath. I sit between his legs and lay my head back on his chest. He begins to wash my chest, this arouses me quickly. He begins to descend lower until he reaches my womanhood. As he caresses me I begin to moan, he kisses my neck and says, "I love you!" I turn around to face him, stare deeply into those beautiful green eyes and say, "As I love you, my king!" I begin to kiss him. He gently raises me up and brings me down on his manhood, I scream out his name as he enters me. He stands up from the tub with himself still buried deep within me, carries me to our bed and finishes what he had started. A few hours later we lie there in each others arms awaiting our sleep. We arrived in Paris the following evening and were greeted by my best friend and her husband. They had arrived here the night before and were already set up in our house. As we are driving back to the house Louisa and I get caught up on all that has been going on. She tells me her son Louis had found his one true love and would be marrying in the fall. I was so excited for them! She asks, "Will you come to England a few months before the wedding and help me with the planning?" I smile at her and say, "I do not think that would be a problem. What do you think, my love, can we make the trip?" He smiles at me and says, "Whatever my queen's heart desires!" We arrive at the house a few minutes later and go inside to get ready for the hunt. I have brought several of my best hunting outfits with me. As I am getting ready Camaz takes me into his arms and says, "My god, woman you look good enough to eat!" I laugh and say, "Later my king, I am starving!" He busts out laughing and says, "Always thinking with your stomach first, I always come in second!" "Yes but just think of how much more you will have to eat later!" He laughs again then pulls me to his lips. A few minutes later we leave the house with our friends and go on the hunt. Paris is so beautiful at night and the food here is abundant and quite delicious! We all sit atop one of the tall buildings in town and are testing the air for our prey. I have caught a whiff of something wonderful off to the east. There are two of them and they are making my throat burn wildly. Louisa informs me she has also picked up scents but they are off to the west. So we take to the sky going in different directions. We have agreed to meet back up at the house after dinner. Soon we are close to our prey, we swoop down and land in a darkened alley. The smell is very close now so I drop down into my hunting crouch and go forward. All of a sudden I feel something strike me in my back. I scream out in pain falling to the ground. Camaz is at my side asking what is wrong. I look up at him with tears in my eyes and say, "I do not know, I was struck by something in my back and the pain is unbearable!" He rolls me over and gasps, I ask, "What is it?" In a angry voice he says, "It is a arrow with a silver tip! I cannot chance removing it here it is to close to your heart! I know this weapon, it is from a vampire hunter's bow. I must get you out of here!" He picks me up and shoots up into the air, just then I hear him cry out. I ask what has happened. He says, "Damn, took one in the leg! But I am fine we have to get you home!" A few minutes later we arrive at our home, the pain is becoming worst, my heart feels like it is on fire! This burn is worst than when I was changed either time and it is getting hotter! I begin to scream out in agony, telling him my heart is on fire. He lays me down on

Our bed on my side and begins to survey the damage from the arrow. Just then Louisa and Richard come rushing in she says, "Oh my god, what has happened?" Camaz explains to them how we were attacked by vampire hunters and the arrow is very close to my heart. He explains it is to close for him to attempt to remove it Louisa quickly removes the arrow from Camaz's leg and says, "Anne I know you are in great pain but we do not have the things here needed to remove the arrow. We are going to have to take you back home so that your healers can remove it." "I do not know how much longer I can endure this burning fire in my heart, I can already feel the pull of the darkness! Camaz, please do not let it take me from you again!" He whispers in my ear, " Fight for me my queen! I will do all in my power to save you!" He gently kisses me. I have not known such pain in all of my vampire years! I lie here screaming and shrieking as the fire scorches my heart. The plane ride did not help either. Several times during the flight I almost gave into the darkness, but I fought it all the way home. It kept whispering to me, saying if I gave in the pain would be gone. But I knew if I gave in the pain of not being with my beloved would be one hundred times worst. As I felt the plane touch down, the jar moved the arrow closer to my heart, I proceeded to scream over and over. I know that we are at the castle now because I can smell all of my family around me. I can hear our head healer speaking to Camaz, he has told him the arrow is to close to my heart and cannot be removed, that I am going to die! I hear my beloved scream out in pain, "No it cannot be possible. There has to be something you can do! I will not lose my one true love! I will not be able to go on without her!" As I lay on the table I feel the darkness begin to take me, blood tears begin to flow down my face, I begin to scream his name over and over asking, "Camaz please please do not let the darkness take me, I love you so much! I do not want to leave this wondrous life you have given me!" I feel him wipe the tears from my face and say in a pained voice, "I am sorry my love but there is nothing we can do, the arrow is to close to your heart to chance removing it. This is tearing my heart from my chest! I cannot lose you, you are my life, my love, my everything!" With that all I feel is the darkness all around me, but I begin to fight, I reach around to my back feel the arrow and scream out, "Never, I will not leave you!" I then yank the arrow from my back. Then there was nothing but darkness

CHAPTER 12

WHERE AM I AND WHERE IS CAMAZ

I am floating in the darkness again! I open up my mind listen for Camaz but I can hear nothing. Oh god I am dead! Removing the arrow has ended my life! It is so dark here and so quiet. I can hear no sound at all, is this to be my afterlife? Just darkness with no sound but my voice in my own head! I must be in hell! But I have done nothing to deserve this, I have only taken the blood of the evil, I have never killed an innocent, I hadn't even done anything before I became vampire to warrant this horrible place! I do not know if god hears a vampires prayers but I didn't care I just began to pray. But if my soul has been damned to hell because I chose to be with my one true love by becoming a vampire then so be it. Oh how my heart ached to hear his voice just one more time but I know this will not be possible because I am dead. In the darkness there is no way of telling time, so it feels like I have been here for years. I am so lonely, I miss Camaz, my family and friends. Oh how I wish I could speak to them again! I begin to cry but I do not feel the tears flowing down my cheeks, so now I know for sure that I am dead. The pain of this fact causes me to call out for my beloved over and over again as the sorrow drags me deeper and deeper. Then something strange begins to happen, I can hear a voice ever so low calling to me off in the distance. I can see a bare glimmer of light off in the distance. I think to myself, has god answered my prayers and is calling me home to him. I begin to follow the sound of his voice pulling me closer and closer to the light. Am I going to heaven, will I get to see all of my family that has passed away again. Will I be able to tell my brother how I avenged his death? Then everything goes bright. I am in a large hall of some kind. There are many around me dressed in hooded long white cloaks. I begin my walk down the aisle to where there is another seated in the middle of them all. I stand before my god for judgment. Then I hear a voice, it is that of a woman! "My child I have heard your pleas and have brought you here." I look up and say, "Are you god? I did not know god was a woman!" She says, "No my child, I am not the god of the human world, I am Cassandra god to all vampires. I have heard your pleas in the darkness and have brought you here to me. For you see, I too once had a true love and I know the pain that you are feeling. I have followed you throughout your entire life with us and you have done nothing to deserve this death. So I have deceived to send you back, but I must let you know, he will not know you when you meet, as the bond will no longer be there. As you know, a paired vampire couple is for life he may not even look at you. You know your former body has been destroyed. I will have to send you back to earth as a newborn, you will have to wait for your coming of age before you can begin your journey back to your one true love. But you will have the power inside you to awaken your former self then you may win him back. If you agree to this I will make ready for your birth, but if you wish to stay here with us then that is your choice as well." I looked at her and say, "I thank you for your invitation to stay, but I want to return so I can be with my beloved again!" "Very well, follow me to your new body." We enter a great room filled with small babies. There are so many here! She walks me to a small bed where I look down on the most beautiful little girl I have ever seen. She has startling blue eyes but jet black hair. She smiles up at me and I feel the bond. Cassandra says, "This shall be your vessel back to earth, take care of this body for it will be your last chance." I then feel myself enter the child's body. I then open my eyes to a brand new life.

CHAPTER 13

MY JOURNEY HOME

I was born to the king and queen of Canada. They were both royals, so that meant I to was a royal. My first few years I grew up a very happy child. But in my third year something began to change, I felt this pull deep within me, so on my third birthday I left home in search of what this pull was. My parents were very understanding but sad at my departure. I follow this pull all the way to Mexico, how strange! I had never even been here before why would I be so compelled to come to this place. I come upon an opening in a cave. The smell of vampire is very strong here but I am not frightened, I feel as if I have come home. Wow, what is wrong with me! At the mouth of the cave I am greeted by a strange looking vampire, he tells me he is the head council for the King and Queen of Mexico and ask, "Are you here looking for an audience with them?" I smile at the nice man and say, "I'm not sure why am here something has just drawn me here." He asks, "May I ask your name young one?" "My name is Annie, I am from Canada my father and mother rule there. He looks into my blue eyes and says to himself, "No way, that is impossible!" "I'm sorry may I ask what you are talking about." "Oh, it is nothing, you just remind me of someone I knew long ago. You even have her stunning blue eyes!" "Oh I'm sorry was it your love?" "No, but was someone very dear to me that lost his one true love three years ago." "Wow I was born three years ago, how strange." He offers to escort me to meet the king and queen. We descend down into the cave and a few minutes later we come out into a cavern. There are buildings everywhere. Why Does this place look so familiar to me! He takes me up a path to a large palace, and says, " This is where the king and queen reside along with our former kings and queen. I will have someone show you to the guest quarters so you can freshen up before seeing them. A very nice lady comes into the room. He says to her, "Maria this is Princess

Annie from Canada she is here to meet the king and queen, can you escort her to the guest quarters please." She smiles at me, takes my hand and says, "Come, your highness this way." I follow her upstairs and into a large room. There are many beautiful things here. She proceeds to ask if I have brought anything with me to dress for our meeting. I tell her I have not brought anything formal with me so she tells me to hold tight she will be right back. A few minutes later she returns with the most beautiful gown I have ever seen. It is emerald green velvet. She says, "Here I think you are about the same size as our former queen, try it on." I step into the dress and pull it up around me. She zips it up. Wow, it fit me perfectly! I was in shock when I looked at myself in the mirror. I loved this dress, but somehow I felt as if I had wore this dress before. How strange this feeling! Maria comes over and tells me to have a seat and she will fix my hair. I enjoyed her brushing my hair out. When she was done I looked in the mirror and my hair had beautiful ringlets down my back. I look at her and say, "Thank you! I love it!" Just then there came a knock on the door. Another woman comes into the room and announces the king and queen are ready to see me. I leave my quarters and I am escorted downstairs and into a large meeting area, I presume this is the throne room. There are two people seated in very beautiful chairs. As I approach them they seem very familiar to me. The man is tall and very handsome with stunning emerald green eyes. The woman is small and petite, she has hazel eyes and long blonde hair. From her scent I can tell that she is a made vampire. But when I look into her face I begin to feel something. Like we have been the best of friends for many years. Just then two more men and a woman enter the room, I feel as if I know them as well, what the hell is wrong with me! Then I look at the man who is alone he is strikingly handsome, he also has those stunning emerald green eyes! All of a sudden my heart begins to soar. I feel as though I have know this man my entire life but how is that possible I don't even know his name. The man and woman go and stand next to the queen the man that my heart sings for goes and stands beside the king. Then my introduction begins. I learn that the king is named Samuel and his queen is Kim. The couple standing next to her is the former king and queen Mikel and Iris. Then I am introduced to the man standing by the King. His name is Camaz and he is a former king and father to Mikel. He smiles t me and my heart really soars! He walks up to me, kisses my hand then says, "I am very pleased to meet you princess Annie. That is a very beautiful name, my wife and love of my life was named Anne. I lost her three years ago." My heart cried out to this man, how sad to lose your one true love! I tell him how sorry I am for his loss. He asks if I would like to go hunting with him, he would show me all of the good spots to hunt. I answer, "Yes I would love to, I am quite hungry!" He took my hand and lead me to the surface. He ask, "Would you prefer to fly or run?" I answer, "Run, I love the feel of the wind on my face!" He turns to me and gives me an odd look. I ask, "What is wrong?" "Nothing, that is what my wife always answered, god how she loved to run!" I see the pain in his eyes, I take his hand and say, "I'm so sorry I have brought up bad memories for you, maybe we should hunt another evening." "No it is alright, I, like you, am very hungry, so let us go." So we began to run, I run as fast as I can to catch him. I am not paying attention to my surroundings and trip on a rock, down I go laughing all the way. He stops and runs back to me then says, "My dear are you alright?" Still laughing I reply, "Yes sir, just two left feet!" " Strange my wife said the very thing to me once!" Something inside of me snaps, all kinds of strange and wonderful memories began to flood my mind. I see our first meeting, our first kiss, my change from mortal to immortal our first night together. I look up at him with blood tears flooding down my face and say, "Oh Camaz, my one true love, I have made it back to you!" He said, "Anne, is that you? How is this possible?!" I smile at him and explain, "When I died I went to vampire heaven, I met our god, Cassandra, she felt it was not my time to come to her but my body had been destroyed when I died. So she sent me back to earth as a newborn. She told me that some day it would all come back to me. But there was no way to know if you would accept me in this new body." He reaches for me and pulls me up. He stares into my eyes, all the way to my soul. He hugs me to his chest and says, "It is not possible, but I saw you in there. Oh my queen is it really you?!" I pull him to my lips and show him that it is me and how much I have missed him! The next thing I know we are on the ground tearing each others clothes from our bodies. He stares down at me with a longing I have not seen since my death. He enters me and I scream out his name over and over with each climax. Once we finish he rolls off of me and we both stare up at the night sky. God, how I love the night! He then rolls toward me and gasps. I ask, "What is wrong my king?" "You have changed! You now look like your old self, I have gotten the complete package back, I cannot believe this!" I say, "My king I am so glad to be back, shall we hunt I'm starving!" He begins to laugh, "That's my girl, always thinking with her stomach!" So off we go in search of our next meal.

## CHAPTER 14

## I AM MYSELF AGAIN

After our hunt we returned back to the palace, everyone gasp when they saw me. Iris and Kim come running up to me screaming, "How is this possible! We saw you die and your body destroyed!" I proceed to tell them of the darkness and going to vampire heaven. How our god had sent me back as a newborn. Kim says, "But the young girl that came to us did not look like you, except for your stunning blue eyes." So I told them how being with Camaz had release me from within the girls body, I just didn't tell them that our lovemaking is what changed me back, that was just a little to private. Makla was due home from college the next evening and was not aware of my return, so we planned a big surprise for her. Camaz told me she had cried for me for months after my death, that even now she still cries for me. I told Camaz I did not want to frighten her so he would break the happy news to her when she arrives tomorrow. The next evening Makla arrived around 9pm, Camaz welcomed her home and told her he had some good news. I am standing in the next room waiting on him to break the news to her, but before he can get the words out she cries out, "Mother!" She rushes into the room where I am. She had caught my scent and knew I was here. She leaps into my awaiting arms and I hug her close to me and say, "My loving daughter, it is so good to be able to hold you in my arms again!" She smiles at me and says, "Oh mother, how I have missed you! I have prayed to god every day for your return and he has heard my prayers! I smile at her and say, "She, she heard your prayers. Our vampire god sent me back to be with all of my loving family!" We visited for awhile then got ready to hunt. Camaz took my hand and said, "Come, my beautiful queen, and sample all the night has to offer!" We take to the sky and start to scent for our prey. Makla has come along with us on the hunt, she does not want to leave my side. It is like old times when we used to take her hunting with us. We arrive back home around 4am, daylight is coming soon so we say our good nights to everyone and head down to our quarters. As I walk into the room I take everything in. God, it is so good to be back home! I go to my dressing table and check all of my things. They are all there as I left them. I turn to Camaz and say, "Oh my love, you have left everything the same as the night I left you." "Yes my dear, my heart shattered that night, but I could not bring myself to remove any of your things from our room. I would look upon them every night before sleep and remember my beautiful queen, I would fall into my sleep and dream of you every night. I think that is what keep me from taking my own life, knowing I could be with you in my dreams every night!" I run up to him and he takes me into his arms and begins to kiss me. I break the kiss long enough to say, "You will never have to dream of me again my love, I will be at your side for the rest of eternity!" He pulls me back to his lips and shows me just how happy he is to have me back home! The next evening I awoke in his arms, I rise up, look into those beautiful green eyes and say, "My love, I want us to go back to our island for awhile. I have gone through so much I just want to spend a few months on the island with us just enjoying each other!" He smiles at me and says, "What ever my true love desires, I shall provide!" I bend down and kiss him, I feel his manhood begin to rise. I look down at him and say, "Hey now, food first I am starving. We have plenty of time for that later!" He chuckles and says, "Always thinking with your stomach, my dear!" We arise from the bed and dress for the hunt. When we arrive back from the hunt there is a great commotion coming from inside of the palace. We rush inside and into the great hall. All of a sudden there is shouting coming from all around us. "Surprise!!!" I look to see all of my closest and greatest friends around us. I look at Camaz and say, "Did you have anything to do with this?" He says, "No my dear, that was all of our daughter's doing!" Just then Makla comes running up to me, hugs me and says, "I wanted everyone to see that you have came back to us and how happy father is!" I hug her to me and say, "I love you my dearest, you have made your mother very happy!" Louisa, Richard, Marylou, our friend Tomas from the Amazon and even Bogden were there, I was happy to see all of them again. We all sit down at the table and I tell them the story of how I had returned from the real death. They were all amazed at my story especially about our vampire god Cassandra. They had heard many tales of her but was not sure she even existed. So, now, they all know she is real. I pray to her every night thanking her for returning me to my beloved! She even came to me one night right after my return, in a dream. She told me she was very pleased with how things had turned out but also warned me to be very careful as she could not send me back again, if I was to be killed. So now as we talk to all of our good friends I think back to when I was taken. That was the most horrible thing I have ever gone through and I will make sure it never happens again. After my party, we say goodnight to all of family and friends and go out to hunt. I tell Camaz about my dream and what Cassandra had warned me of. He stared into my eyes and said, "I promise you that you will never be alone, I will always be with you, and if I cannot the elite squad will be." I say, "I know you will protect me with your life my love, but I am still frightened!" He pulls me to is chest and says, "Do not fear my queen, nothing will ever happen to you again. You are mine and will be for all of eternity!" The following evening we left for the island. I was so excited, I could hardly wait until I could walk in the sun again! But then I got to thinking, even though I am myself again we have not shared blood, does that mean I will not be able to walk in the sunlight or did our mixing of blood come back when I did? Camaz looks at me and says, "What are you thinking about, my queen?" "I was just thinking about going out in the sunlight, I do not know if it is possible now. We have not shared blood in this body." He looks at me lovingly and says, "I will not chance it to find out, we will stay out of the sunlight, it would only take a few minutes to destroy you!" Now I am sad, I had so wanted to walk with the sun on my face, but he is right, we cannot chance it. We have been on the island now for almost a month, even though I cannot go out into the sunlight I still have enjoyed every minute of the moonlit beaches and swimming in the ocean with Camaz. We still lie on the beach but instead of staring up at the sun we take in the beautiful moonlit nights. One evening when we return from our hunt I began to feel very strange. I tell Camaz I am not feeling very well and go to lay down. He comes up to me and asks, "What is wrong my queen?" "I do not know. I feel as though I have eaten something very bad and my stomach is upset. That is not possible is it?" He thinks for a minute and asks, "My dear, how long have you been having these feelings?" "I don't know, about a week I guess, why?" He looks at me and says, "Impossible! You are made, not born!" I ask him what he is talking about. He says, "My dear, you sound like you are in the early stages of pregnancy!" I look at him in disbelief and say,

"What! That is impossible. I was made, not born." I think for a minute, then it hits me like a ton of bricks. I smile at him and say, "Wait, when I came back Cassandra said I would be born to two pure bloods! That means I am born not made! My god, I am pregnant!" He takes me into his arms carrying me around the room. I have never seen him so happy! He then says, "A child from our own union! My love, I am so happy. I did not think it was possible and now our child will be coming in a month!" He places me on the bed, tells me he is going for takeout, that I need my rest. I laugh at that and say, "Oh goodie, can you bring back Chinese please!" He busts out laughing and says, "Yes my love, even if I have to go all the way to China I will bring it to you!" He leaves, I hear the speedboat leave the dock. Lucky for me there are plenty of Chinese in Mexico City. Even Mexicans have to have their Chinese food! About an hour later he returns, he is carrying a small Chinese man in his arms. I can smell the wonderful evil coming off of the man. Camaz has knocked the man out. He lays him on the bed and says, "Here, my love, feed, you need to keep up your strength!" I move the man's head to the side and strike, drinking down. As soon as I am done the sick feeling returns. Camaz smiles and says, "Do not worry yourself, my queen. The sick feeling will be gone in a few more days." He was right too, in two days the sickness was gone and has never returned. I am now into the second week of my pregnancy, I am beginning to show, I look in the mirror at my growing belly and smile to myself. I think to myself, I hope it is a boy! I would love to give my true love an heir from my body and not some surrogate! Even though Makla is next in line for the throne but she would not be king, she would need to find someone to rule with her. She has told me many times she does not want to rule. The next evening when we arose Camaz went to ready the boat for our trip home. He told me he wanted me home so I could be well taken care of. I smile up at him and say, "You are all the care I need, my love!" He kisses me gently and heads off to the boat to make ready for our trip back home. I am going to miss our island, even though I did not get to walk in the sun this time, I still remember all of the times that I had. A few minutes later Camaz returns, picks me up and carries me to the boat. I say, "Silly, I can walk, you do not have to carry me!" He smiles down at me and says, "I am not taking any chances." He places me in the seat on the boat and we head back home. God, I am going to miss this place!

CHAPTER 15

OUR CHILD IS COMING

Two weeks later I have grown heavy with child. I can feel the pull telling me it is time for the delivery. I smile at Camaz and say, "My love, it is time!" His eyes light up with joy. He takes me up to the third floor for the birthing of our first child together. I have been told that the mother does not want anyone around her when it is her time, but I cannot bear the thought of being away from Camaz. I have asked him to stay with me. He smiles at me and says, "If that is what you wish, I will not leave your side!" I can now feel the baby coming, my whole body is aching, not from pain but from joy! I cannot wait to hold our child in my arms! I suddenly have the urge to push. The next thing I know the child is out. It is a little boy, I reach for him bringing him to my chest. He has Camaz's jet black hair but my blue eyes, I say, "Wow, look at that, his eyes are blue!" Camaz takes his son into his arms. While he is holding our child I bite the umbilical cord and I push one last time to release the afterbirth. Camaz is sitting, holding his son to his chest and singing to him! Wow, he sounds so great. I tell him I am going to take a bath and I will return. I walk into the bathroom with a smile on my face. After my bath, Camaz tells me he is going down to announce the birth but first he asks, "What will we call our son?" I look up at him, smile and say, "Camazotz." His whole face lights up. He reaches for Camazotz. I place him into his father's arms and he leaves to announce his son's name for all to hear. A few hours later I have rested enough to start receiving callers. The first to come in is my best friend, Louisa. She comes up to me, hugs me and says, "Oh Anne, he is so beautiful! I still cannot get over those stunning blue eyes!" I smile at her and say, "Neither can I. I had thought they would be like Camaz and yours. I was shocked when I saw them. Oh Louisa, he is so perfect!" "My dear friend, I am so happy you where able to feel the joy of giving birth, there is nothing like it!"

Then Camaz came back into the room, carrying our son. He placed him into my arms and said, "Sweetheart, I think he is ready for his first meal." Louisa tells us she will be right back. A few minutes later she returns with a bottle. I can smell the glorious scent . She tells me it is fresh from the host and hands the bottle to me. I place it at his lips and he begins to suck A few minutes later he has finished every last drop and has fallen off to sleep. I stare down at his sleeping face and my heart sings! Camaz has brought a small cradle into our room and has placed it next to my side of the bed. I sit up and place our sleeping son into it. He tells me he has dinner waiting for me in the other room. He will stay here with the baby while I dine. I leave the room, the man is sitting in a chair in our sitting room. I can see the fear in his face. I walk up to him turn his head and strike. His warm blood begins to flow down my throat. Once I have finished him I head back into our bedroom. Camaz smiles at me and asks, "Did you enjoy your dinner, my love?" I reply, "It was alright, but you know how

I do love the chase!" "Soon my love, we will take to the air and then the chase will begin." He lies down beside me, takes me in his arms and says, "Thank you for what you have given me, my happiness, my life and now my son!" He pulls me to his lips and kisses me ever so gently, I fall asleep in his loving arms. A few days later I am ready to hunt. Louisa is going to stay with the baby, so I know he is good hands. His Auntie loves him to death! I am feeling rather sexy tonight so I go to my closet and take out my special leathers for the hunt. After I have dressed Camaz comes into the room to see if I am ready. He smiles at me and says, "Wow, my dear, you look so good. You are making me so horny I just want to rip that off of you and make mad passionate love to you!" I smile at him and say, "When we return, my king, I am ready for the chase and I am starving!" He burst out laughing and says, "Always thinking with your stomach, my queen!" We leave the castle and run off into the beautiful night. I love the feel of the wind on my face and the smells of the night. When we reach the edge of the forest we take to the air. A few minutes later we arrive in town. We land on top of a building. I close my eyes and let my sense of smell take over. I test the air for my prey. Soon I pick up something that smells wonderfully evil. I look at Camaz, smile and leap to the ground. He follows right behind me. I begin to stalk the wonderful smell, letting my nose lead me to my prey. It is getting stronger as we go down the dark street. Then I stop, I test the air one more time and say, "There, in that house. There are four in all two men and two women and they are all evil!" I can tell that they are mated couples, two are in one bedroom the other two in another. We enter the house and head upstairs. We enter the first room, Both are sound asleep in the bed. I go to the man, he goes to the woman. I whisper in the man's ear, "Wake up. I have come for you, you are mine!" This jars the man awake, he looks at me. I smile, showing my fangs, causing him to begin screaming. This has awoke the woman, she begins to scream as well. We strike at the same time and drain them dry.

Just then the other couple comes running into the room. The man yells, "What the hell is going on in here?!" I look at the man and say, "Just that. Hell. Welcome to your worst nightmare!" I leap on the man knocking him to the ground. Camaz has done the same with the woman. She is fighting for her life but it will do no good. He slams her head to the side and strikes. I have the man's head pushed toward them so that he can see his evil mate die. Once I see the life leave her eyes I strike draining the man dry. I release his lifeless body look to Camaz and smile. He smiles back at me and asks, "Well, my dear, are you full or shall we hunt more?" I say, "No I am quite full and I am ready to go home so we can get to the part where you remove my clothes!" We leave the house, he takes me into his arms and leaps into the air flying me all the way back to the castle. Once we are in our quarters we go into baby Camazotz's room to check on him, he is out like a light. We tell Louisa to have a good evening and she leaves the room. We head back to our room for some undressing. In seconds he has both of us undressed and gently pushes me down on the bed. I stare up into those beautiful green eyes and say, "I need you my king I am burning way down low and only you can put out the fire!" We have not made love since I became pregnant so I am more than ready for him. He is raised up on his arms above me staring down at me, I can see the lust in his eyes. He begins to lower himself towards my womanhood but he waits to enter. I begin to claw at him, my passion has taken over and I cry out, "Now, please! I need you now!" He enters me. I begin to scream his name over and over as he thrusts in and out until he brings me to full climax. My extreme passion has now sparked in him, faster and faster he goes until he explodes. He lies there on top of me for a few minutes still deep within me. He slowly withdraws making me scream again in ecstasy. He rolls over to his side of the bed and we both lie there panting wildly. He rolls onto his side, stares into my eyes and says, "My god, woman what has gotten into you? I have never heard you scream that much before!" I smile at him and say, "I guess it was just the heat of the moment my love!" He chuckles and says, "Woman, you are amazing! I love you for all that you are!" I roll over, he takes me in his arms and I drift off to sleep.

## CHAPTER 16

## CAMAZOTZ'S FIRST BIRTHDAY

It has been one year since the birth of our beautiful baby boy. He is a striking little man! He so reminds me of his father. He has a loving heart and gives his all in everything he does. Camaz is teaching him the art of hunting tonight, I watch as my two men stalk their prey. I am perched high above them on a building, I test the air and pick up on the prey they are stalking. I take to the air and follow close, they come to a house where the scent is the strongest. There are two men on the front porch smoking cigarettes and drinking. Camaz approaches the porch and asks if he can use their phone, that his car has broke down and needs to call for a tow. The two men invite him into the house, little Camazotz is following close behind. Once inside I hear the men begin to scream, then silence. Just then I catch a whiff of something delicious. I let my sense of smell take over. The smell is coming from a few houses down. Without thinking I take to the sky in search of that wonderful smell. I land in front of the house, I can tell there are two evils inside, one is a woman. But I also pick up on the scent of three innocents upstairs, one is a child. I leap to the second floor and enter a window. I begin searching for the innocents. I enter a bedroom and find the two adults tied up on a bed, but the child is not with them. The two are in very bad shape as they have been beaten very badly. I pick them up one at a time and take them from the house. Once I have hidden them I go back into the house to find the child. I enter through the same window and let my nose lead the way. Soon I pick up on the child's scent. I begin to follow it until I reach the room, I open the door and to my horror it is a little girl about 10 years old. She is tied up on a bed and I can tell she has been raped. I see the tears flowing down her cheeks. I pick her up from the bed and whisper in her ear, "Do not be afraid little one. I will have you out of here and safe in just a minute." I leap from the window carrying her. I take her to the hiding place where I have hidden the other two.

Tell them to stay put that I am going for help. But I have no plans

on leaving this place, these two are going to pay with their lives! I

go back into the house and begin my search for the evils. My

blood has already begun to boil just thinking about what they

have done to that poor child! I hear them downstairs so I creep

down to the lower level. The man and woman are in the kitchen

making something to eat. I am so angry now that I am seeing red.

How dare they act like nothing is wrong after what they have

done to that child! I stand in the doorway and say, "Good evening

you two, enjoying yourselves are you?" They both turn around

and say, "Who are you and how did you get into our house!" I just

laugh and say, "It was quite easy I came in through an upstairs

window, but I rescued your captives before coming down here.

Now let me tell you what we are going to do, you are going to

take off running then I am going to hunt you down like the sick

animals you are!" The man says, "Your crazy, lady! I will kill you!" He comes at me with a knife. I smile at him showing my fangs. He stops dead in his tracks and says, "What the hell are you!" I smile at him again and say, "Why, silly boy, I am a vampire and I am very hungry!" They both take off running out of the house and into the street. I so love the chase so I give them a few minutes start then go after them. I take to the sky so they do not see me coming. I soar above them just watching them running for their lives. But I am growing tired of the chase and I am starving! So I swoop down pick up the woman and carry her into the air. I sink my fangs into her neck and begin to feed. Oh my she was so sweet! I drop her lifeless body and go after the man. I am going to have some fun with him! By the time I am done with him he will be screaming for death! I swoop back down and grab him. I carry him off toward the woods. Then I pick up Camaz's voice in my head. He is looking for me I tell him I am alright and heading to the woods with my prey. He tells me he will meet me there. I land in a clearing and release the man. I proceed to tell him what I plan on doing to him. tell him, "First, I am going to rip your eyes out, then I am going to rip your heart from your chest just as I finish draining the blood from your body. For what you have done to that poor innocent child you shall suffer!" I leap on the man knocking him to the ground. As I promised I, ripped his eyes out. He is screaming over and over in pain. I push his head to the side and strike. His warm salty blood begins to flow, I drink, and right before his heart stops I withdraw, look down him, and thrust my hand into his chest grab his heart and tear it from his body. In a few minutes Camaz and our son arrives, He looks at me and says, "My, my, he must have been a very bad man to anger you this much, my queen!" I look up at him and say, "Anyone who would do what this man has done to a child deserves to die in the manner I chose!" He reaches for me and says, "Come, my queen, let us go home, our son is ready for bed and I am in need of you!" We arrived back home around 4am, we took little Camazotz to his room and got him ready for bed. He smiled up at me and said, "I love you Momma!" "As I love you, my son!" We both kissed him goodnight and headed for our room. Once inside he takes me in his arms and says, "My dear, you are so beautiful, god, how I love you! You are my life, my love, my own!" I smile up at him and reach to kiss him. But something was not right. He just didn't seem to be into the kiss. I pull back and say, "What is bothering you my king? Have I done something to offend you?" He hugged me to him and says, "Never, you would never offend, me my love, it is just that I must go away for a few days and I do not like leaving you behind. I promised I would never leave you alone again after what happened. I would take you with me but I know you will not leave our son for that long." "But dear, I will be fine I promise. I will not hunt alone, I will take the elite guard with me if I have to, I promise!" He pulls me back to his lips and kisses me with all of his passion. A few hours later I lay in his arms with a smile on my face. Oh how I love this man! He makes me so happy! I thank Cassandra for sending me back to him right before I fall off to sleep.

## CHAPTER 17

## CAMAZOTZ'S SECOND BIRTHDAY

It is now little Camazotz's second birthday. He is growing into a fine young man. He is tall and muscular like his father but I am still stunned by his beautiful blue eyes. He is out in the courtyard right now training with his father in the fine art of fighting. Camaz is teaching him to use a sword he is becoming quite good with it! I watch my two men with great pride. Camaz turns to me, raises his sword to honor me, I smile down at him. He says, "Come, my love, it is your turn to teach our son with the daggers." This is something I have become quite skilled at, he has even told me I have become better then he. I leap from the balcony and land in front of them. I go to where the weapons are located, pick up two daggers then come back to where Camazotz is standing. I hand one of the daggers to him. I begin instructing him on the art of fighting with the dagger. I show him how to fend off an attacker and turn to deliver a fatal blow. I explain to him that with any creature of the night you must either strike the heart or the neck with the blade. We practice a little long then Camaz asks, "Are you hungry, my love?" "Yes, as a matter of fact, I am starving!" "Then let us hunt!" We all left the courtyard and headed off toward the woods. We began to run through the woods, I just love the wind on my face! Then all of a sudden Camaz stops dead in his tracks scents the air and yells, "Ghouls!" Oh shit not that again. I turn and start to run but before I can take to the air I am knocked to the ground. I am now fighting for my life! If this thing bites me it will send me into madness again, there is no way I am going through that again. Then I feel the weight of the ghoul lifted off of me. I roll over just in time to see my son rip the beast's head off. He runs over to me and asks, "Mother, are you alright? He did not bite you did he?" "No, son, I am fine. The beast did not bite." He reaches for me and helps me up. We look for Camaz and find him in battle with three ghouls.

He is moving so fast it is hard to keep up, but I know if he slips they will get him. We race to his side I leap on one of the ghouls, Camazotz on the other tearing them away from Camaz. I pull my daggers from their sleeves and drive them into the ghoul's neck then pull them free slamming them into the beast's heart. Camazotz has done the same, god he has learned quickly! That's my boy! I run over to Camaz he is lying on the ground looking up at me. The ghoul lies beside of him, the head missing. I check his body for bite marks but can see none. I ask, "Camaz are you okay? I have not seen any bite marks please tell me the ghoul has not bitten you!" He smiles up at me and says, "No, my warrior queen, I am fine. Did you see our son! He was amazing!" I laugh and say, "Yes, takes after his mother!" "That he does, my dear!" I reach down to help him up. When we arrive back at the castle we ask our son what he would like for his second birthday. He smiled at us and said, "I have heard Mother and you speaking of an island where you love to go, I would like to visit that island."

Camaz smiles at our son and says, "And so you shall, my son."

The following evening we took the speedboat out to our island.

We all played in the ocean for hours but now sunrise is coming.

We must get inside how I wish I could still go out in the sunlight!

But we can not take that chance, for this was not my original

body. We all go inside the house. Camazotz, wants to stay up for a

bit, but we warn him not to go out into the sun. We do not know if

we have passed on the ability to go into the sunlight to him. We

head to our room to get ready for sleep. While I am getting

undressed I ask Camaz, "Do you think it is possible that at least

you have passed on the ability for him to go out in the sun?" "I do

not know, my dear, I have not been in the sun since I lost you and

have no need to because you cannot go with me." He takes me in

his arms staring into my eyes and says, "You are my life, I will go

no where that you can not be with me!" He kisses me

passionately. A few hours later I fell to sleep knowing this man

would do anything for me. The next evening when we awoke

Camazotz was waiting for us. We had told him yesterday about the sunken ship we had found and he wanted to go explore it. So we all ran out in to the surf went under the water. We swam for a few miles and came upon the ship. We entered and began to explore. We had already found the treasure a few years back but we let our son look for it. Camaz had came to the island a few days before our trip and placed the treasure chest back on the ship so Camazotz,. could find it. We told him what ever treasure he finds would be his. He enters the captain's quarters and comes back excited. He tells us he has found treasure. We go in with him to see his booty. Camaz picks the chest up and carries it off the ship. We swim back to the island. He places the chest on the table and says, " Open it my son, what ever is inside is yours to keep!" I must say for a 12 year old this was very exciting! He runs over to the chest, breaks the lock with his bare hands then opens it. Inside was the treasure we had found. We had no need for it so had just put it away in a exciting! He runs over to the chest, breaks the lock with his bare hands and opens it. Inside was the treasure we had found. We had no need for it so had just put it away in a closet not knowing our son would some day find it. He smiles at us and says, "This is all mine! Really!" "Yes, my son, it is for you to do with as you please." He picks up the chest and takes it into his room. Camaz takes me into his arms and says, "You have a good heart, my queen. I have never seen our son happier!" He kisses me gently. We would spend a few more days on the island and head back to the mainland. I love our island but I was ready to get home.

CHAPTER 18

CAMAZOTZ'S COMING OF AGE

Today should be a very happy and joyous day, but I am sad. Today is Camazotz's third birthday and his coming of age. The three years have flown by to quickly but I must let him go. He will be proclaimed an adult tonight in his coming of age ceremony. He has grown into a strapping young man. He is as tall as his father and is built like him. His black hair is at his shoulders and any woman would lose herself in those stunning blue eyes. I am so proud of our son! I have just finished dressing for his party when Camaz comes into the room. He comes over to me and takes me in his arms. He says, "My god, woman, you are absolutely beautiful tonight. But why are you so sad?" "Oh, Camaz, our son will become a man in a few short hours. I just wish we could have spent more time with him!" "But my dear he is not going anywhere, he will still be here with us. Stop worry yourself and let's get down to our son's party." He releases me, takes my hand and leads me downstairs. All of our family and friends are here for his coming of age party. We walk to where my best friends are sitting. I take a seat beside Louisa. She smiles at me and says, "Oh Anne, it is so good to see you again. My, has Camazotz grown!" "Yes he has, I am so sad though He is a man now and soon will be looking for a bride." Camaz has gone to the front of the hall and makes the announcement that his son has now become a man. He raises his glass to our son and toast his long and happy life. He returns to our table and takes the seat beside me. We watch our son go out into the crowd to meet with his friends. A few hours later the head council proclaims him an adult and the heir to our kingdom. Some day our son will sit upon the throne and rule our country as we have. After the party we go out hunting. Camaztoz. has gone off with his friends to hunt, so it is just us. He asks me where I would like to hunt this evening. I tell him I feel like running. So off we went into the beautiful night in search of our next meal. I am running like the wind having a wonderful time trying to catch Camaz, but he is still just too fast for me. As usual I miss judge my steps and stumble to the ground. Camaz runs back to me laughing and says, "I swear, woman, you are the most clumsiest vampire I have ever seen!" He reaches for me but I yank him to the ground with me. I roll him onto his back and sit atop of him. I look down into those stunning green eyes then say, "I may be the world's clumsiest vampire, but I am yours!" I bend down and begin kissing him madly. Before I know it he has rolled me over on to my back and is staring down at me. He says, "You know that I will love you for all of eternity, you are my one true love and there can be no other!" He begins to undress me, the fire between my legs is building. I watch as he removes his shirt. I reach up and run my hands down his stone hard chest marveling that this man is mine and will be for all of eternity. I smile up at him and say, "As you are my one true love, I have loved you since the first time I laid eyes on you and have never looked back!" I pull him down to me kissing him madly. I feel him enter me and I scream out his name over and over again. Afterwords we lie there staring into the night sky. God, it is so beautiful! I have always loved the night, even before I was made vampire! Camaz raises up on one elbow and asks, "Well, my beauty, are your ready for dinner?" "Yes, my love, I am quite famished!" "Then let us take to the sky for the hunt!" We quickly get dressed and leap into the air flying off toward the next town. As we are flying I pick up on a strange scent I look at Camaz and point down so we can land. I tell him of the scent I have picked up. It is a vampire that I have never met before. Camaz test the air and replies, "I know not of this vampire either, my dear. Shall we go introduce ourselves to him?" "I don't know, I still remember the last strange vampire I ran into and do not what to take a chance." "I understand your concern my dear, but we must find out who he is and why he is here. I will be right by your side, I promise no harm will come to you!" We start walking toward where we had scented the vampire. We spot him in a clearing, he has his prey on the ground and is draining him. He hears us coming and jumps up into a defensive stance. Camaz holds up his hand and says, "We mean you no harm, stranger, we were just out hunting and came upon your scent. You are new to our lands, so we just came to say hello." The man relaxes, walks over and Introduces himself. "Hello, my name is Stan, I am from the United States and have come here because I have heard the prey down here is very plentiful." Camaz says, "Welcome Stan, my name is Camaz and this is my wife, Anne. Welcome to our beautiful country!" "Thank you very much and I must say you are a very lucky man, your wife is stunning!" "Thank you, that she is. Come and we will take you to our home so you can met the rest of our coven. I pull at Camaz's hand and say, "But my dear, we still have not hunted and I am starving!" He smiles at me and says, "We shall go back to the house, we have plenty of food to please my queen!" The man says, "You are the king and queen?" I say, "We were, but not now. When we arrive at the castle we will

Introduce you to the current king and queen." So we head off to

the castle with our new friend. I am feeling very uneasy about this

man, I do not know why but something is just not right. I have

always been able to tell when I am in danger and my radar is

going off left and right. When we arrive at the castle I tell Camaz

there is something I need to discuss with him about our trip. He

looks at me strangely and says, "Stan, can you excuse us, it seems

my wife has more planning for our up and coming trip? Just make

yourself at home we will return soon." I pull at his hand taking

him into another room. He says,"What is wrong, my love?" "I am

not sure but my radar is going off telling me that I am in danger!"

Camaz sends me to our room as he does not want me in any

danger. He will keep me updated in my head with all that is going

on. He heads to the room Stan is in He begins to talk to Stan, "So

Stan, whereabouts are you from in the United States?" "I am from

Montana sir, why do you ask?" Camaz takes a second to alert me where the man is from. Then says to the man, "My wife has family in the states and I was just wondering where you were from." Then they begin to speak of other things. I have entered Camaz's mind so I could listen to the conversation. This is something we have learn recently, a gift Cassandra has given me. While I was in vampire heaven she told me I would have some special gifts that she would be sending me back down to earth with. We found out by accident one evening while we were hunting. Camaz was upstairs when I entered his mind I could hear everything he was saying and what the human was saying as well. So far that is the only gift that has manifested itself. I listen closely as the man tells that he has lived in Montana all of his life and he was born to royals there. He told Camaz his brother had been here on a trip and had loved it here. That there was so many beautiful women in this country. He has come searching for a bride. I scream out to Camaz in his head, "Oh my god, he is that rapist's brother! Please do not let him take me from you!" In his soothing voice he says, "It is alright my dear, if this is true he will not get anywhere near you. But we do not know for sure I will need to have the council investigate this man and see if he is related to your abductor. I will be down in a few minutes my dear." He excuses himself telling the man one of the staff would be right in to show him to his quarters, and that we will be going for our dinner now. A few minutes later he is in our room with me. He pulls me to his chest and says, "I am so sorry, my queen, you are so frightened. Shall I have your meal brought to the room?" "No, it is okay, as long as I am with you I know I will be safe. Let's eat!" I pull at his hand and lead him from the room. First we go to the council chambers and speak with Astor. We explain about the strange vampire and where he is from. We ask him to run a background check on the man to see if he is the brother of the vampire that kidnapped me. Astor told us he would get on it right away. We go down to the holding cells to select our dinner.

CHAPTER 19

I SMELL A RAT

The following evening when we arose, I got dressed in my battle gear just in case, I placed my sword in it's sheath and my blades on my arms, I covered my sword with my long flowing hair, I wore long sleeves to conceal my blades. They are wide enough for me to have quick access to my blades. Camaz comes up to me and says, "My dear, you do not have to go upstairs if you do not want." "My love, I can not be afraid for the rest of my UN-dead life. I will not let anyone ever take me from you again!" He pulls to me to him and kisses me gently telling me how proud he is of me. We go upstairs and find Stan in the living room. He is sitting at a table and is talking with Astor. We go over and say our hellos and ask to speak to Astor. We excuse ourselves and head to the council chambers, once inside we ask Astor what he has learned. He has found out the the man is of royal blood. His mother was a princess from the southern states and his father a prince from the northern ones. They have been living in Montana his entire life. He has one brother and two sisters. That is all he has learned so far. He would give us more information as soon as he receives it. I am still very frightened that this is the brother of the man who kidnapped me and has come to take his revenge on me for his brother's death. The pain and horror of my rape is still fresh in my mind even after all these years. I know if it is found out that this is the brother of my rapist and is here to get revenge, Camaz will tear him to pieces! We return to the living room and tell our guest we are going out for dinner and will return soon. I do not want this man any where near me until we know for sure he is not the brother of the rapist. We leave the castle and take to the air. We land in a field right outside of town. I catch the scent of my prey and begin to stalk him. Camaz is close behind. I hide behind a tree and watch my prey as he is attacking a woman, he has her down on the ground and is tearing at her clothes. I begin to see red with the pain so close to me, I leap from the tree knocking the man to the ground. I am on him so fast he has no idea what is going on. I slam his head to the side and strike. Suddenly the woman comes to, sees what I am doing and begins to scream. I raise up from my meal, blood dripping from my fangs. I say to the woman, "Please, do not be afraid I will not harm you. I have come for him and he has paid with his life for all he has done to you." She begins to cry and asks, "I am so grateful for what you have done, but what the hell are you?" "My dear, I am a vampire, but we are not like the vampires of folk lore We only feed on the most evil of humans, like this piece of trash. You have nothing to fear from me!" "I want to tell everyone what a wonderful thing you have done for me but no one would believe me." "I am sorry child but I cannot take that chance. There are many vampire hunters out there searching for my kind. They will destroy us if they get a chance. Now, I want you to look deep in my eyes, when you awake you will not remember me or what we have discussed. Do you understand?" She replies, "Yes." I took to the air leaving her behind. I feel bad about doing the mind trick on her, but I must protect our lives. I find Camaz not far from where I have fed He has his meal on the ground draining him dry. I land next to him. He looks up at me and smiles and says, "Well, my, dear, it looks like you had a very good meal." "Yes my love, but I am ready to go home now. I am still having this feeling of dread." He stands up takes me into his arms and flies me back home. When we arrive at the castle we meet up with Astor, we ask where Stan is. He tells us he has gone out hunting and said he would be back later. We say goodnight to Astor and go down to our quarters. Once behind closed doors he asks me, "My dear, are you sure these feelings you are having are about him?" "I don't know for sure, but I do know I am frightened!" "Very well, my queen, from this moment on I will not leave your side, even in the hunt. I will not allow anyone or anything to harm you. I will protect you with my life!" I smile up at him and say, "I love you!" He takes me in his arms and kisses me passionately. A few hours later we fall off to sleep in each others arms While I sleep I dream. We were out hunting when all of a sudden we are attacked by vampire hunters. We are surrounded and I have taken an arrow close to my heart again. I fall to the ground screaming. I then see my beloved take an arrow directly in the heart. He falls to the ground dead. As I lay there dying I see our god Cassandra, She says to me, " My child, your fear of the man is unfounded. It is not he you should be fearing but the vampire hunters. They are in your lands searching for all vampires. This man will help you to fight the hunters. Please do not fear him, for I have sent him to protect you." I abruptly awake from the dream screaming. Camaz grabs me and holds me to him the blood tears are flowing down my cheeks. He says, "It is only a dream, dear heart, you are safe here with me!" I look up at him, he wipes the tears from my face I then tell him about the dream and what our god Cassandra had told me about Stan. Then I told him about the hunters being here in Mexico look for us. He tells me to get dressed that we need to go to the council then our elite squad to make ready for the vampire hunters. Once upstairs we meet with Stan. We tell him what is going on and that we need his help. He smiles at me and says, "My lady, it would be an honor to fight beside of you!" Once we have met with the council we leave the castle and head to Cristos to make our guard ready for the attack. Everyone is there and are awaiting our instructions. We ask Stan if he has ever been in battle before. He tells us that he has fought in several wars between the Northern and Southern states. We take him the the weapons room and give him his choice of weapons. We then chose the section of countryside to search for the hunters. We all take ff in different directions. Stan has come with us, along with Dempie's son. I feel very safe with them with us. My fears of this man no longer plague me for our god has told me that she has sent him to protect me. We take to the trees as we have heard voices off in the distance. As we look on we see a group of about twelve men, all armed with weapons used to destroy vampires. We listen to what they are saying. They have learned where our cavern is and there are many more hunters on their way there now. We must get back to protect our family and friends. But first we must take out these hunters so they will not be a problem. The arrow in my chest from my death still burns vivid in my memory. I must be very careful around these men! We make our plan of attack but Camaz does not want me to come. I say, "I cannot let you put your life in danger and do nothing. I have sworn to protect you with my life and I will!" I take to the air, Camaz and Stan are right behind me. We look down on the men They are unaware that we are right above them. I draw my sword from my back and make ready for the attack. We all swoop down on the men taking them by surprise. I take out two of them with my sword. I am now on the ground going after another. He turns, raises his bow and fires an arrow at me. I hear Camaz scream "No!" I shoot straight up in to the sky. I feel the arrow strike me in the arm. I scream out in pain as the burning begins, but I have no time to worry about this minor wound. I swoop back down and take out the man before he can pull his bow again. I look to my left and see Camaz in battle with three of the hunters. He moves so fast they do not see him. Quickly he has beheaded all three. We run to where Stan is. He is embattled with two hunters but seems to be holding his own. So we go after the other four. They are now running for their lives, for you see, Dempie's son is chasing them. I watch as he takes down two and doesn't miss a stride as he chases the other two. He gets one of them but the other is getting away! I take off running to catch the man. Camaz yells for me to stop, but the blood lust has taken over. I chase the man down and knock him to the ground. He raises a silver spike and tries for my heart but I stop him in mid swing, snapping his arm like a twig. He screams out in pain dropping the spike. I rear back and strike. I begin to drink him in, but then something happens to me, I roll off of the man and begin to heave like I am going to throw up. I begin to scream for Camaz he comes running over to me. I look up at him and ask,

"What is wrong with me? I feel so strange, I feel as though I am going to be sick!" "My dear I tried to stop you but the blood lust had you. You have taken the blood of an innocent!" I look at him odd and say, "How is that possible? He was trying to kill me!" "But my dear they only kill vampires. They do not take the lives of humans, so they are innocents as well. Your body is craving his blood but our blood oath is causing you to feel sick. It will take several days for it to get out of your system." He reaches for me and helps me to my feet. He looks at the arrow embedded in my arm. He says, "My dear I must remove the arrow but it will be very painful!" At that, he reaches for the arrow and removes it from my arm. I scream out in pain, I can still feel the burning of the silver. He takes his shirt off and wraps it around my arm to slow the bleeding. We take to the air heading back home to help with the fight there. Thank goodness the arrow did not hit my sword arm, so I am still fit for battle. When we Arrive at the entrance to our home it is complete chaos. There are vampire hunters everywhere. They are in battle with our elite squad, who is protecting the entrance to our home. There are many dead from both sides e swoop down and land in the heat of the battle. I run at one of the vampire hunters that has one of our elite on the ground and is getting ready to deliver the fatal blow. I leap and kick him from off of our man. He rolls and is back up on his feet. He comes running at me with a vengeance, swinging his sword. I sidestep the hunter, turn and take him out with one blow of my sword. I turn to confront the hunter in front of me. He is a tall man of about six feet, he is very muscular with tattoos on both arms. He has his bow drawn and is taking aim at me. I watch as the arrow leaves the bow, I only have a split second to avoid the arrow. I leap straight up into the air as fast as I can. The arrow goes whizzing by just missing me. But he has drawn another and is getting ready to release it. I drop back down to the ground and take off running but he has released the arrow. I brace myself for the hit but it does not come. I hear someone behind me scream out in pain. I turn to see Stan go down, the arrow is embedded in his chest. I run at the hunter, remove his head before he can draw another arrow. I run back to Stan, I look down at him I can see the life leaving his eyes I and ask, "Why did you do that? You have given up your life for me and you don't even know me!" He smiles at me and says, "Dear woman, I was sent here by our god with the sole purpose of protecting you." I drop to the ground beside of him, take his hand and tell him, "Thank you Stan. You are a brave and mighty warrior I will always remember what you have done for me!" I watch the light leave his eyes. As he lays there dead I begin to cry for my brave protector. All of a sudden I hear my beloved cry out my name in my head. He has been wounded, I must get to him. I take off running toward where I last saw him in battle, screaming the whole time in my head that I am coming. I spot him on the ground. There are three hunters, two have him pinned to the the ground the other has his sword raised and is about to deliver the killing blow. I scream in horror and run at full speed toward the man with the sword. I withdraw my daggers from their sleeves and throw the first at the man's sword arm. The blade digs deep into his shoulder causing him to drop his sword. In seconds I am on this man, I slam my other dagger deep within his heart. He falls to the ground dead. The other two hunters have let go of Camaz and take off running. I look down at Camaz, he has many wounds all over his body, but he also has a arrow embedded in his chest. I can tell it is not near his heart, but it needs to be removed I bend down and tell my beloved that I must remove the arrow from his chest. He smiles up at me and says in a weak voice, "My warrior queen, do as you must, but if I do not make it know that I have loved you from the first moment I laid my eyes upon you. I will always be with you even in death!" I begin to cry and say, "Do not say that! You will not leave me! I will not allow it!" I remove the arrow from his chest. He screams out in pain. I open up a vein in my wrist and allow my blood to flow into the wound it begins to seal at once. I pick him up and run inside. Once inside I take him down to out quarters and take care of the other wounds. He is still very weak so I offer him my neck. He bites down gently and begins to drink. I am beginning to become weak from the blood loss and my own wounds. He can sense this and stops feeding. I say, "No my love, you need to feed more, you are still very weak!" He looks at me and says, "No I will take no more of your blood you are to weak, my love. You need to feed. I will be alright until you return!" I kiss him tenderly on the lips and tell him I will be right back. I leave our quarters to go to the holding cells to feed. While on the way there I meet up with Astor. He tells me all of the hunters have been defeated. But we have lost many in the battle. I tell him to take care of all of our wounded, that I must feed so that I can heal Camaz. I reach the holding cells and quickly drain three. I am so full I can hardly walk but I must get back to my beloved. I quickly run back to our rooms go up to where he is laying, and look down at him. I can notice that he is starting to look better, but he is still very weak. I sit down beside him and offer my neck again. He pulls me to his mouth and bites down, I can feel my blood begin to flow. A few minutes later he withdraws and pulls me to his lips kissing me passionately. I break our kiss and say, "Is my king feeling better?" "Yes my love that I am. Tell me how the battle is going." I tell him the battle is over and we have lost many warriors but I am not sure who they are. I tell him the story of how Stan had protected me with his life. He looks at me and says, "Wow and you were so afraid of him in the beginning!" I tell him, "When you are better my love I want to make the trip to Montana to take him home to his family." He smiles at me saying, "My queen, you have such a good heart. Do you think you will be able to handle being there after what has happened to you in the past?" "I do not know, but what I do know is that I owe it to him to take him home to his family!"

## CHAPTER 20

## MY RETURN TO MONTANA

We arrived at the Billings airport three days later to bring Stan back to his family. We had contacted his mother and father the day after the battle to inform them of his death. I told them how bravely their son had fought and how he had saved my life. We were met at the airport by two of their elite and taken to their home. There we were introduced to Stan's parents. His father was named Stan as well. he was a very handsome man with black hair and hazel eyes. His mother was named Sophia. she was small framed with beautiful blonde hair and big blue eyes. The sadness in their eyes were heartbreaking!. We all sat down at the table and I told them the tale of our great battle and how brave their son was. I told them he jumped in front of the arrow to protect me. Sophia told us that Stan's funeral will be tomorrow and they have the guest room ready for us. She asks if we are hungry. I tell her,

"Yes, but I have never hunted here before. I have been here only once." I left it at that but she could see the pain in my eyes. She takes my hand and says, "Come, my dear, we have plenty of food here. There will be no need to go out." I look back at Camaz, he says, "Go, my dear, I will follow shortly." Once we are in their holding rooms she asks, "What is bothering you, my dear?" I proceed to tell her of my abduction and rape. She says, "That is terrible! Do you know the name of this rapist?" I say, "Yes his name was Jack." She gasps saying, "Are you sure he was from here?" "Yes, that is what he told me. Why?" She looks at me with sad eyes and says, "My husband's brother was named Jack. He has been missing for years." "I am so sorry, but when he took me my husband found us in a cave in the Rim. He told me that since Jack had raped me it was my right to kill him. I took his head in that cave." "My dear, your husband was correct. A female vampire has the right to take the life of any vampire that takes them by force. We will not speak of this again. I do not want my husband to know his brother is dead." Just then our men walked into the holding cells. Camaz looks at me and asks, "Have you fed yet my dear?" I tell him no we were just getting acquainted, but I was ready to eat. We each went into separate cells and had our meals. We returned upstairs, said our good nights and retired to the room they had prepared for us. Once behind closed doors I told Camaz about our talk and how I had found out that Jack the rapist was Stan's brother. I asked, "Do you think our god Cassandra, sent Stan to protect me because of what his uncle had done to me?" "I do not know, my dear. I am just glad he was there. I do not know what I would do if I lost you again! I do not think I would be able to go on without you!" He takes me in his arms and kisses me madly. The following evening when we awoke we got dressed to attend Stan's funeral. There were many in attendance, but we were unfamiliar with most. When it came my turn to speak I stood before him and told all how he had stood by me and had protected me with his life. That he was a dear and close friend that I would miss very much. After his funeral we went on a hunt, we were invited by his sisters. The princesses Carolina and Frances, I enjoy their company very much. They told us great stories of their brother's battles during the wars between the North and South. I have invited the girls back to our country for a visit and they have agree to return with us in a few days. As we stalk the streets of Billings, Camaz has picked up a scent. He tells us there are four men in the house below and they all smell of evil. We all land on top of and into the street. I so love the chase so I give them a few minutes start then go after them. I take to the sky so they do not see me coming. I soar above them just watching them running for their lives. But I am growing tired of the chase and I am starving! So I swoop down pick up the woman and carry her into the air. I sink my fangs into her neck and begin to feed. Oh my she was so sweet! I drop her lifeless body and go after the man. I am going to have some fun with him! By the time I am done with him he will be screaming for death! I swoop back down and grab him. I carry him off toward the woods. Then I pick up Camaz's voice in my head. He is looking for me I tell him I am alright and heading to the woods with my prey. He tells me he will meet me there. I land in a clearing and release the man. I proceed to tell him what I plan on doing to him. tell him, "First, I am going to rip your eyes out, then I am going to rip your heart from your chest just as I finish draining the blood from your body. For what you have done to that poor innocent child you shall suffer!" I leap on the man knocking him to the ground. As I promised I, ripped his eyes out. He is screaming over and over in pain. I push his head to the side and strike. His warm salty blood begins to flow, I drink, and right before his heart stops I withdraw, look down him, and thrust my hand into his chest grab his heart and tear it from his body. In a few minutes Camaz and our son arrives, He looks at me and says, "My, my, he must have been a very bad man to anger you this much, my queen!" I look up at him and say, "Anyone who would

Do what this man has done to a child deserves to die in the manner I chose!" He reaches for me and says, "Come, my queen, let us go home, our son is ready for bed and I am in need of you!" We arrived back home around 4am, we took little Camazotz to his room and got him ready for bed. He smiled up at me and said, "I love you Momma!" "As I love you, my son!" We both kissed him goodnight and headed for our room. Once inside he takes me in his arms and says, "My dear, you are so beautiful, god, how I love you! You are my life, my love, my own!" I smile up at him and reach to kiss him. But something was not right. He just didn't seem to be into the kiss. I pull back and say, "What is bothering you my king? Have I done something to offend you?" He hugged me to him and says, "Never, you would never offend, me my love, it is just that I must go away for a few days and I do not like leaving you behind. I promised I would never leave you alone again after what happened. I would take you with me but I know you will not leave our son for that long." "But dear, I will be fine

I promise. I will not hunt alone, I will take the elite guard with me if I have to, I promise!" He pulls me back to his lips and kisses me with all of his passion. A few hours later I lay in his arms with a smile on my face. Oh how I love this man! He makes me so happy! I thank Cassandra for sending me back to him right before I fall off to sleep.

CHAPTER 21

HOME AT LAST

We arrive back at the castle at around 10pm the following evening. We take the girls up to the guest quarters and leave them to unpack. We then go to visit our son. He is in his room listening to his music. I go up to him, he hugs me and says, "Welcome home Mother, I have missed you!" "As I have missed you my son!" Camaz then asks him if he would like to go hunting with us later. He replies, "Not tonight father, I am going out with friends for dinner." We tell him to have fun. We leave his room and head for ours. I go to my closet to select my hunting outfit for the evening. I come out with my full leather bodysuit and high heel boots. Just as I begin to dress, Camaz grabs me from behind, spins me around and looks deeply into my eyes. He says, "Woman, you look so stunning in that outfit! Any man would give into you alive or dead!" He begins to kiss me. I soon break our kiss and say, "Later, my love, I am starving. Shall we hunt!" He laughs and grabs my hand, pulling me from the room. A few minutes later we have taken to the air and are heading toward the city. Just before we reach the city I pick up on a strange scent. It is of some supernatural creature I have never smelled before. I say to Camaz, "What is that? I have never smelled that scent before!" He tests the air for a minute and says, "I'm not sure my dear, I have never smelled such a creature before." So we go down to investigate. We land in a field right outside of town. We begin to track the smell staying low so not to be seen. We come upon a creature that stops us in our tracks. It is about six feet long with 6 tails and is massive. It almost looks like a fox but something is different about it. It has long flowing silver hair all over his body. Its face looks almost human, but it has long sharp fangs and claws. It seems to be searching for something. Soon I pick up the scent of an evil. He is only about a mile away, it seems the creature is stalking this man. We follow behind the creature staying upwind of him so he is not alerted to our presence. We spot the man at a campfire. We watch as the beast begins to stalk

him. Its hunting is so beautiful to watch. Its movement is almost

silent, but because of our keen hearing we pick up on it. It leaps,

knocking the man to the ground. The man begins to scream, but

not for long. The beast rips his throat out then begins to devour

his prey. I step on a twig, trying to get closer to the beast. I have

alerted it. It looks right at us, roars and charges. We both jump

Straight up into the air and hover above the beast. It then speaks,

"How dare you interrupt me while I am feeding! What kind of

demons are you, I have never seen the likes of you before?" I yell

down to him saying, "We are not demons. We are vampires and

like you, we only hunt the most evil of humans. We are sorry we

have disturb, you but you are new to our country and we have

never before seen the likes of you. What type of creature are

you?" He smiles up at me showing all of those razor sharp teeth

and says, "I am a Night Kitsune, I come from Japan. I have lived

for over 200 years. I have come here to hunt as I have heard the prey is plentiful." Then something very strange happened, it changed into human form. I stood there staring in disbelief. I ask, "How did you do that? Are you like the werewolf?" "No, my child, I am a beast of the night that has the ability to shape shift into human form." Camaz asks, "May I ask your name sir." "I am Kimsu, and what may I ask are your names?" "I am Camaz, former King of this country and this is my wife Anne." "I am very pleased to meet both of you." Camaz asks Kimsu if he would like to come back to the castle with us. He tells us yes but he is still hungry and would like to continue to hunt. We tell him he can come with us as we have not had our dinner yet. He shape shifts back into his fox form and off we go into the night in search of dinner. While hunting, we tell him the hunting here is very good but that we also go to other countries to hunt. We tell him if he would like to stay we would take it up with our council to have him proclaimed a member of our court. He tells us he would be honored and he had always yearned to be apart of a family. But his kind was very rare and he had not located others of his kind. So that is how we met the newest member of our family. Later on, he would turn out to be our best asset. It is now early spring everything is blooming and smells so wonderful. Tonight we have chosen to hunt in the city as I am in the mood for city food. As we stalk the dark streets I ask Camaz, "My dear what do you think about taking a trip to England? We promised Louisa and Richard we would visit the last time they were here." He smiles at me and says, "If that is what your heart desires, then I shall take you there!" All of a sudden I pick up on a wonderful scent, I say, "Oh goodie! Dinner!!" He laughs, and we take to the air following that delicious scent. A few minutes later we arrive in town and set atop one the building. I let my senses fan out searching for our prey. I pick up on it quickly, off to the east. I point in that direction and we take to the air again. We soon come upon a house in the rundown side of town. We land in a nearby alleyway, and come around the front of the house. can tell from the scent there are three inside. Two are evils and one is an innocent. I send Camaz

around to the back of the house and have him await my signal. I

walk up to the front door and knock. Soon a man comes to the

door and asks if he can help me, I tell him that I have lost my way

and could I use his phone to call friends. He invites me in and

says, "Follow me the phone is in the kitchen." When we reach the

kitchen the other man is seated at the table and is reading the

newspaper. He looks up from his paper and eyes me up and down.

I can see the lust in his eyes. As I go over to the phone the man

that let me in grabs me from behind, I scream out, this is my

signal to Camaz. The man knocks me to the floor and is on top of

me tearing at my clothing. The other man has joined him and is

holding my arms above my head. Camaz strolls, casually, into the

room. He says, "My, my. Looks like you boys are having a party,

may I join?" The one on top of me turns to him and says, "Sure

the more the merrier!" He goes back to undressing me. By now

the blood lust has taken me over completely. I break the other man's hold on my arms and send him flying into a wall. I reach for the man on top of me, he looks at me in astonishment and says, "How in the hell did you break free of him?" I smile at him, baring my fangs, and say, "Well, let's see, I am over 100 times stronger than any man on earth and oh yes, I am also a vampire!" He begins yelling for Camaz to help him. Camaz comes up to the man and says, "Why would I do that? My wife is quite hungry!" Then he goes after the other man. I slam the man's head to the side rear back and strike. My fangs dig deep into his throat and the blood begins to flow. I drink him down, savoring every drop. Once finished, I stand up, wipe the blood from my mouth and go to where Camaz is finishing his meal. I look down and watch him finishing the man off. He looks up at me, smiles and says, "My beautiful queen, have you had your fill for the evening?" I answer, "Yes, my love, I have for blood, but my body desires something else that only you can provide!" "Then shall give you what you need!" He rises from his meal, picks me up into his arms and carries me outside. He leaps into the air and we fly back

home. A few minutes later we arrive at the castle and he carries

me down to our quarters, kissing me the whole time. He closes

the door behind us and begins to undress me He takes me into the

shower and washes my body. God, how I love him to wash me! It

sends shivers of delight down my spine. Once we are done

showering, he dries my body and carries me back to the bedroom,

lies me down on the bed and begins to kiss me. Starting at my

lips, then my neck then all the way down. As he reaches my

womanhood, I scream out his name. The orgasm racks my body,

causing me to tremble with joy. He begins kissing his way all the

way back up to my lips. I breathe him in, his scent drives me

crazy with desire. I break our kiss and say, "Please, baby, I need

you so badly! My whole body is aching for you!" He stares into

my eyes and smiles, then he enters me. I scream my pleasure over

and over with each thrust. Afterward, we lie in each others arms

in complete bliss. I drift off to sleep with a smile on my face. The next evening when we awake, Camaz goes to make plans for our

trip to England. While he is gone I go to my closet to select the

outfits I will be taking with me. As I look through my hunting

outfits I think to myself, "My, it is about time to go shopping for

new clothes." I know that there are many shops in London for the

type of things I need for the hunt so as soon as we arrive and are

settled in I will go shopping with Louisa. About an hour later

Camaz returns to tell me everything has been made ready for our

trip. We will be leaving tomorrow evening. I tell him I want to go

shopping in London when we arrive, I need new hunting outfits.

He smiles and says, "I can hardly wait to see you in them!" He

takes me into his arms and kisses me tenderly. I break our kiss

and say, "Let's hunt, I am quite hungry!" Tonight Camazotz,. and

our newest member Kimsu, are hunting with us. The two of them

have become quite good friends. They are always together even in

the hunt. We leave the castle and run through the woods. Oh how

I love to run! I am always trying to catch Camaz but he is still just

a bit faster than me. But, boy, can Kimsu run! He has passed
Camaz like he Is standing still. All of a sudden I catch something,
stop and test the air. I have picked up on the scent of something
very evil, but it does not smell of humans. I look at Camaz and
say, "I smell something, but it is not human! But what ever it is, it
is not vampire either!" Camaz tests the air and says, "No, it is not
human, but at one time it was. I know this scent, it is a werewolf."
I ask, "But how is it I did not smell the werewolf?" He says,
"Because he is so evil it is masking his werewolf scent. I was only
able to tell because I have been around for hundreds of years and
have known many werewolves." Kimsu then speaks, "I have
never smelled something so evil! Shall we go take care of him?!"
We take off into the woods in search of this evil beast. We come
to a clearing and spot the beast. He stands over seven feet tall and
is massive! Suddenly all of my memories begin to flood my mind.
I become very afraid of this beast. Camaz can see my distress so
he pulls me to him and tells me it will be okay, that he will not

allow the beast to get anywhere near me. Just then, the beast

scents us. He stands up from his kill and roars .I look at the body

on the ground, it is of a young woman. The pain on her face and

her body being ripped to shreds sets something off deep inside of

me! I feel the anger building within me. My blood begins to boil.

I no longer fear this werewolf, I draw my sword from behind me

and make ready to attack. Camaz grabs my arm to stop me. I look

at him, he says, "No, I will not have you putting yourself in

danger, my love. We will take on the beast." I say to him with my

eyes blazing red, "No! We shall attack together. This beast is

going to pay for what he has done to that woman!" "Very well,

my love, but stay close to my side. I will not lose you to this

beast!" We all charge the beast. He roars in defiance and attacks

Camazotz,. but our son is too quick for the beast, he sidesteps him

and turns readying himself for the next attack. Just then, Kimsu

leaps at the werewolf knocking him to the ground. The beast roars

out in pain ane slings Kimsu off of him. Kimsu slams into a tree and is momentarily stunned. The beast has now set his sights on me. He runs at me, draws those massive claws back and swings at me. He catches me across my chest. I fall to the ground, screaming in pain. The claws have dug deep and the wounds are bleeding profusely. I hear Camazotz scream, "Mother!!" I see him run at the beast, but the beast is ready for him. He grabs Camazotz in his massive paws and pulls him to his mouth! I scream out for Camaz to save our son. I see him streak passed me and he is on the beast. Camazotz drops to the ground, rolls and comes back up ready to attack the beast, he has his sword drawn. I watch as my love does battle with the beast. He has the beast down on the ground with his hands around his massive neck. The beast rakes his long claws across Camaz's back and I hear him scream out in pain. The werewolf is now up heading for me. I try to get up to take to the air but the blood loss is just too much. I close my eyes and ready myself for death. But it does not come, I open my eyes just in time to see Kimsu tackle the beast to the ground and proceeds to rip the throat out of the beast. Camaz runs over to where I am laying, picks me up and leaps into the air with our son right behind him. I can tell my love is becoming very weak from blood loss. I look at our son and say, "Son, your father is getting to weak to carry me much further." He then reaches for me and takes me from his father's arms. We arrive back at the castle and Camazotz carries me down to our quarters, lays me down on the bed and says, "I am going back to check on Kimsu then I shall return." He closes the door behind him. The claw marks are deep in my chest, Camaz opens up a vein and begins to flow his blood into the wounds. I say, "No, my love, you are to weak to proceed. You need to feed!" "Astor is bring food as we speak, so you have no need to worry, my love." I can feel the wounds begin to close on my chest. Astor comes into our room with two men. He brings the first over to me and says, "Drink, Anne!" I pull the man to me and strike, drinking him down. Camaz has the other man and is draining him as well. I am beginning to feel better so I go to Camaz and begin the healing process on him. I open my wrist and allow my blood to flow over his wounds. Astor has left the room, so I offer my neck to Camaz, he gently bites down and begins to drink. After a few minutes he releases his hold on my neck and offers me his. I bite down and begin to drink. His blood is so very sweet! It took us a few days to recover from the werewolf's attack but as soon as we were well we left for our trip to England.

CHAPTER 22

LONDON VACATION

We arrived in London around 2 a.m. and were met at the airport by Louisa and Richard. On our ride back to their home we girls did some catching up. I told her about our new friend Kimsu and what a wondrous creature he is. She said she would like to meet him the next time she came home for a visit. I told her how well Camazotz was doing in college and that he would be done in a few months. She told me their youngest daughter, Sabrina would also be home from college in a few months as well. I told her we needed to go shopping, that I was in need of new hunting attire. She told me she had found the perfect place and would take me tomorrow evening. After dinner we returned to their castle and retired for our sleep of death. As I lie in his arms, Camaz says, "Are you happy my love?" "Yes, very much so. I am so glad we came for a visit!" He rolls to his side, staring down at me and says, "Have you ever regretted me changing you?" I look at him puzzled and say, "Why would you asks such a thing?" "It's just that you have been through so much, my dear. I feel the blame for all of it!" I pull him to me saying, "Silly man. When you ask me if I wanted to live in the night, all those years ago, I never hesitated in giving you my answer and never looked back! I was born to be a vampire and I will love you for all of eternity!" I preceded to show him just how much I loved him. The following night when we arose I got ready for my shopping trip with Louisa. We arrived at a small shop deep in the heart of London. As we look around the shop I am amazed at how much leather is in here. I pick out three outfit and go to the dressing room to try them on. I come out with the first a skin tight pair of leather pants and halter top. I am pleased when I see the look on Camaz's face. He says, "My vampire goddess, you look good enough to eat! No man will be able to resist you in that outfit!" I smile at him and head back into the dressing room to try on the next outfit. After our hunt, when we are back at the castle, Camaz tells me the first outfit is his favorite and wants me to wear it for him the next night on our hunt. A few days later, Louisa and Richard tells us they have received word that a man has been killing woman and he has been called the ripper because of the way he has been copying the murders of Jack the Ripper. Little did we know this was no impostor, it was the evil man himself and he was vampire! As we search the streets of London for our prey, I suddenly pick up on a scent. I begin to follow it until we reach an alleyway. The smell of evil is very strong in there. I can also smell the sweet scent of an innocent as well. I tell Camaz I am going to have some fun, and enter the alley. I can see the man. He has a woman down on the ground with a knife at her throat. He is readying for the killing blow. I clear my throat to get the man's attention. He turns to look at me, I am startled. His eyes are glowing bright red. He leaps to his feet and charges me. I scream for Camaz, the man has knocked me to the ground and is on top of me. He smiles, showing me his fangs. I see a flash beside him, then he is flying through the air and slams into the wall. Camaz is standing in front of me in a protective stance. He says, "If you come any closer to my wife I will rip your head off!" The man stands up shakes the dirt from himself and says, "I am not afraid of you, your wife is the one that interrupted my feeding. But I must say, she is quite beautiful. You are a very lucky man." Camaz says, "That woman is an innocent but yet you kill her! How could you!" The man smiles at what he has said and answers, "I have always taken the innocent. I follow no ones rules! For, you see, I am Jack the Ripper!" I scream at him, "That is impossible. He does not exist any more. He has been dead for hundreds of years!" "That is where you are wrong, my dear, for I am he!" He leaps into the air and disappears I look at Camaz and say, "We have to stop him! We must go back to the castle for our battle gear then hunt him down!" "My dear, we are not familiar with this place. He could be hiding anywhere!" "Then we will get Richard to help. He has lived here his entire life! We must stop that man. We cannot allow him to continue killing innocent women!" So we take to the night sky, back to talk to Richard and Louisa. We arrive there a few minutes later. They have just returned from their hunting trip. We tell them we have something to discuss of the utmost importance Richard says, "Then come, let us discuss this problem." We enter library and go over everything we have learned about Jack the Ripper and the fact that he is killing innocent women. A few hours later, Richard has assembled his elite guard and we are readying ourselves to search for this madman. It is a little after 1am so we only have a few hours before sunrise. I am dressed in my battle gear. I have pulled my hair up so that I have ready access to my sword. We all take to the air and go off in different directions to search for the Ripper. Camaz is close by my side, I know he will protect me with his life but can still see those burning red eyes in my mind. God, the pure evil just permeated off of that madman! I just cannot fathom what would drive a man to hate women so much. Suddenly I catch a whiff of him. I look at

Camaz then point off to the east. We begin to follow his scent until we reach the outskirts of town. We land in a small clearing in the woods. His scent is making my throat burn wildly. I have never smelled such evil before! We begin to search the area for Jack. I point to an area off to the right and make a circle with my hand for Camaz to go around. I begin to walk toward the wonderful smell. Just then, Jack leaps from a tree knocking me to the ground. I am on my back fighting wildly, I cannot reach my sword so I take him on in hand to hand combat. He is very strong, but I have become quite skilled over the years. I raise my knees up into his chest and toss him off of me. I quickly get to my feet and reach for my sword bringing it around in front of me. I make ready for his attack but before he can charge me again Camaz is on him. I see Camaz swing and Jack goes flying into a tree snapping it in half. He is quickly back on his feet charging at me again. But Camaz is to fast for this madman. He leaps at Jack knocking him to the ground. I am now standing over him with my sword drawn I look down at him and say,"For all of the innocent women life's you have taken, I shall take yours!" I swing downwards severing his head from his body. We arrive back at the castle a few minutes later to let everyone know Jack the Ripper had been destroyed. Richard sent messengers out to let his elite know to return to the castle. Once in our quarters Camaz takes me in his arms, stares into my eyes, and says, "You still amaze me after all of these years my warrior queen! You are so brave. That is one of the reasons I love you so much!" I smile at him and say, "You are the one, my king, that makes me feel brave! You are so strong and true. That makes me feel as though I could take on the world! I love you!!"He says, "As I love you!" He pulls me to his lips showing me just how much he does love me! A few days later we are readying ourselves for our trip back to Mexico. We have all decided to hunt together one last time before we head for home. I am going to miss my best friend! As we stalked the dark silent streets I think back to all of the wonderful times Louisa and I have had hunting. We have always made a great pair for the hunt! We now sit atop a high building scenting the air for our prey. Suddenly Louisa catches something. She looks to me and smiles, leaps into the air. We follow close behind. She soon sets down on a deserted street. Drops down in her hunting crouch and begins to stalk her prey. I also have picked up on that wonderful sent and my throat is a blaze. I can tell there is at least six of them nearby. At the end of the street there is a large Victorian house with lights on through out. There is four men and two women inside, they are all evil. I test the air for the scent of innocents but cannot find any. Louisa and I go to the front of the house, the men to the back. I have a plan! I tell Louisa to smear dirt all over her body, I do the same. We are going to tell them we have been attacked and need help. God how I love the game! Once we have made ourselves look be-shelved I go up and knock on the door. A few minutes later a man answers, he looks at the both of us and says, "My god, what has happened to you two!" We proceed to tell him of our attack and that we need to call the police. He invites us into the house. We follow him into the living room. Two men and one woman are sitting there. The man begins to tell them what has happened to us. I have alerted Camaz we are now inside, so they enter from the rear of the house. I can tell the other two people are in an upstairs bedroom and are having sex. One of the women in the living room asks, "Would you ladies like something to drink, while we are waiting on the police?" I say, "Sure, that is very kind of you." I know the police have not been called, for you see, I have seen the lust building in the men. A few minutes later, the woman returns with two cans of soda, handing them to us. We thank her then sip at them acting like nothing is wrong. The fire has begun to burn wildly in my throat! I do not know how much longer I am going to hold back while we play our little game. I can tell that Louisa is so ready for the kill. All of a sudden there comes a scream from upstairs. This is our cue, I leap from the couch, knocking the woman that brought us the drinks to the ground. She screams at me, "Hey get off of me!" I stare down at her and smile baring my fangs for her to see. I can now see the fear in her. I slam her head to the side, and strike, her wonderfully evil blood begins to flow, putting out my fire. I look to the side to see Louisa on one of the men. I watch as she rears back and strikes. But the other man is going after her! I leap from my prey and take off after him, knocking him into a wall. He hits so hard that he is stunned momentarily. The other woman has taken off running out of the house. I yell to Camaz that she is getting away. He goes after her with a vengeance. I watch as he gracefully takes her down, as if he is a large lion taking down a gazelle. Just then the man gets his senses back rises from the floor pulling a large knife from his belt. I am not paying attention to him because I am watching Camaz. He comes running at me and drives the knife deep within my chest. I scream out in pain and go down. The man is now sitting on me and is getting ready to slit my throat. I close my eyes readying myself for death. I feel his weight lift from me. I open my eyes and see Camaz tearing the man apart. He runs over to me, checking the wound in my chest. He says, "Thank god the knife was not silver! I was so afraid that I had lost you again!" He bites his wrist and allows the blood to flow into my wound. I can feel the wound begin to close. He takes me in his arms and we leave the house. As he carries me back to Louisa and Richards home, I look up at him and say, " What is it about everyone mortal or immortal wanting to stab me in the heart! What have I done to deserve this!" He laughs, "I guess they all love you to death my queen." In a few days I was fit as a fiddle and ready to get back to our beloved home. We say our goodbyes and we will keep in touch. We leave for the plane. Once on board I fall off to sleep in my loving husbands arms.

CHAPTER 23

CAMAZOTZ GREAT SUPRIZE


I awoke to the feel of our plane touching down. I roll over and stare into those gorgeous green eyes and smile. He pulls me to him and says, "Welcome home my queen!" He kisses me tenderly. A few minutes later we are dressed and disembark the plane. Camazotz is waiting for us. He tells us he has some exciting news, but wants to wait until we are home. About 30 minutes later we arrive at the castle. We quickly go inside and are greeted by all of our family and friends. Kimsu comes up to us and says, "Welcome home sires, we have missed you!" I smile at him and say, "As we have missed you mighty Kimsu!" We hug for a minute and Camazotz says, "Come Mother and Father. I have someone I would like for you to meet. He leads us into the living room. There on the couch sat a stunning girl with long flowing brown hair and big blue eyes. From her scent, I can tell that she is human. Camazotz is beaming! He says, "Mother and

Father, I would like to introduce Michelle, my fiance." I smile at her. Walk up, take her hand and say, "Welcome to our home Michelle, my name is Anne. I am very pleased to meet you. This is my husband and Camazotz Father Camaz." Camaz takes her hand and kisses the back of it. He smiles at her and says, "I am so happy that our son has found someone to love! I hope you two will be as happy as we are my dear." Later we learn that Camazotz had already told her what we are and that she didn't care. That she wanted to be with him and if it meant becoming as us, then so be it. We all discussed her change to our life and it is planed for two days from now. They are to wed in a month. I get my girls together and start planing the wedding. Maria will be making Michelle's gown for the wedding. That evening we go into town for dinner. I have dressed in one of my new outfits I got while in London. It is a full bodysuit of black leather. I have thigh high spiked boots on that match. Camaz tells me that I have never looked more sexy. I smile at him and say, "Only for you my king.

There can be no other!" He takes me in his arms and kisses me tenderly. I break our kiss and say, "I am starving! Later my love!" He laughs then we take to the air. I catch a scent off in the distance and begin to follow it. A few minutes later we set down atop a building in town. I let my sense of smell fan out, to locate that wonderful smell. A few streets over I smell the aroma of pure evil. I point in the direction the smell is coming from and we take to the air again. Soon we come upon the house where the smell is the strongest. We land in front, scenting the air. There are two men inside but there is also two innocents. I send Camaz around to the back and I go up to the door and knock. A man of about six feet and very muscular answers the door. He looks at me in my leather outfit and says, "Why are you dressed like that? Are you going to a costume party?" I say to him, "Why no silly, this is my hunting outfit." He says, "And just what are you hunting, a good time?" "As a matter of fact, that is exactly what I am hunting. May I come in?" He smiles at me and says, "Sure, come on in."

He yells to his friend inside that they have company. The other man enters the room. He is a short squat man of about 250 pounds. He smells as if he has not taken a shower in years. But the evil coming off of him smells oh so sweet! He eyes me up and down. I can see the lust building in his eyes. The man that answered the door tells him that I am here for a good time. Then asks if he wants to join in. With that, Camaz walks into the room. He has already alerted me that he has rescued the women from upstairs, so let the party begin! He says, "Good evening gentlemen, I see you have meet my wife. Gorgeous isn't she and oh how she loves to play games!" The both say at the same time, "Who the hell are you? Get out of our house!!" I turn to the man that invited me in, smile at him baring my fangs. I say, "Let the party begin!" I leap at him, knocking him to the floor. He is fighting me with all of his might, but it is like a kitten trying to fight off a pit bull! Camaz has his prey on the ground and is already draining him. I look into the frightened mans face and smile. He sees my fangs and screams. I smack him, telling him to shut up. I rear back and strike. His warm, sweet, salty blood begins to flow. It is so evil it drives me into a feeding frenzy. I savor every last drop! I raise up from his growing cold body, and wipe the blood from my mouth. I look at Camaz and say, "My, my, was he ever so sweet!" He chuckles and says, "Are you ready to go home now my love? I am so ready to get you out of that outfit!" "What ever my king desires!" So we leave taking to the air heading back home. Once we are behind closed doors, he comes up to me lifts my hair, and slowly begins to lower the zipper in my bodysuit. As he does, he is kissing down my back the whole way. I turn to face him. He pulls the fabric from my shoulders downward, exposing my breasts. He kisses my right nipple. He goes down to remove my boots. He removes the rest of my outfit. I stand there in the moonlight, naked for him to see. He begins to remove his clothing. He removes his pants and stands there naked. I marvel at his body. I think to myself, "My god, this man is mine for all of eternity!" He walks up to me, takes me in his arms and says, "You have the most beautiful body human or otherwise, I have ever seen in all of my 900 years! God, how I love you!" I smile at him and say, "You know that kind of flattery will get you anywhere with me, my one true love!" He pulls me to his lips, kissing me madly. He picks me up caring me to our bed. He lies me down and stares into my eyes. I can see my soul in those yes! He enters me. I scream out his name over and over telling him how much I love him. A few hours later we lie in each others arms panting wildly. He rolls over onto one elbow, staring into my eyes and says, "Woman, do you know how happy you have made me all of these years! From the moment I laid eyes on you, my heart sang and has been singing every since!" I smile up at him and say, "I love you!" We fall off to sleep with smiles on our faces. That night I dreamed of the future. I see our son's marriage, his crowning as king and their long rule as King and Queen of our domain. This was one of the best dreams I have ever had! I see our god Cassandra, she comes up, hugs me and says, "It is good to see you again my child and see how happy you are back with your one true love! But I have come to warn you, there is a great upheaval coming and your entire family is in danger! They will come from the east so be prepared!" I say to her, "Who Cassandra, who is coming?" With that I abruptly awaken, screaming her name. Camaz pulls me to him, telling me that it was only a dream. I look at him with tears running down my cheeks I proceed to tell him of the wonderful dream I had about our son, but then I told him of Cassandra's warning. Of how we where all in danger. He pulls me to his chest and in a soothing voice tells me, "There, there, my dear, I will not let any harm come to you or our family!" We go to the council to alert them of my dream and what Cassandra has warned me about. So they sent out scouts to the four corners of our country to find out if anything was coming. Later that evening we made ready for Michelle's transformation. I explained the process to her and that we would all be here for her during the burning. Camazotz has decided to make the change himself, to make their blood bond even stronger. I watch as he goes to her, gently stroking her face, telling her how much he loves her. She turns her head exposing her neck to him, I watch as our son strikes then recoils just as quickly. He has left the gene behind so her burning began. During the next two days, she screamed over and over for death but he was right there by her side letting her know that everything was going to be alright. He so reminded me of his father when I had endured the blistering fire both times. So strong, so loving! Then I hear her heart take it's final beat. She opened her eyes to a brand new world. She smiled up at Camazotz and said, "I love you. My god this so amazing! But why does my throat fell like it is on fire?" He smiles at her and says, "That is the thrust my dear. You need to feed before it becomes unbearable!" I look at Camaz and say, "Wow. That is what you said to me when I first felt the fire in my throat!" He laughs at that and says, "That it was my dear!"

The children leave the castle and run into the beautiful night in search of her first meal. After the children have left we go to council chambers to see if they have found out anything as of yet. Astor is there waiting on us. He tells us that he has received word back from the east that there is rumors of an uprising with the ghouls. I think to myself, "Oh shit, not them again! Will this war with them never end!" I look at Camaz, he can see the fear building in my eyes. He hugs me to him and says, "Do not worry my love, I will never let them get near you again! I will take you from this place to our island where I know you will be safe!" I yell, "No! I will not leave your side my love. I will not have your life in danger while I sit back and do nothing!" He says, "My brave warrior queen, I will not ask you to risk your life for me! I am sworn to protect you and that I shall." "But I to am sworn to protect you also my king, I will not leave your side! We will not speak of this again!!" He smiles saying, "Very well my love, but I will not leave your side for any reason!" He takes my hand and we leave the council's chambers. We go to our chambers and dress in our battle gear. We are going to Cristos to gather all of our elite guard and make ready for the horror that is coming. Dempie Junior meets us at the door, telling us that all is in preparation for the battle. He takes us over to a group of men. I can tell they are all fairy warriors. He introduces us to them one by one. We go to met with our werewolves. There leader Charles, has them all ready for the battle. We meet with Stantos to make sure all of our vampire warriors are ready. We learn that the leader of the ghouls is the brother of the one that almost ended my life with the sword at my neck. He has amassed an army, hell bent on destroying all of us, especially Camaz and me. Soon we leave Cristos and head back to the castle with all of our elite guard. We arrive about an hour later. We have the werewolves outside the entrance to our home and they will guard us during the day. The rest of us go below to ready the rest of our family and friends. Our great friend Kimsu, has just returned from a trip to the middle east and I am so please that he is here to help. I tell Camaz that I am going to go gather up all of the women and children, and take them to the special hiding place. Once I have them all inside and safe I return to be at Camaz's side. Just then Camazotz and Michelle enter the room. They are in a heated argument. She does not want to go below, to the hiding place, but stay with him. She is newly born and has not been trained in combat yet. I go up to her and say, "My dear, I know how much you want to stay and help, but you are not trained in combat as of yet, if you where to stay, you would be endangering him. He will try to protect you! Please come, let me take you below." We receive word that the ghouls have entered our lands and are on the way here. I quickly take Michelle down to our hiding place and leave her with the other woman and children. I go back upstairs and make ready for battle. Camaz tells me when the ghouls arrive, to stay close to him, so I do not get separated from him. I hear a great roar coming from the entrance to our kingdom. It is the werewolves, alerting us the ghouls are here. I reach behind my back and retrieve my sword. The rest of our elite guard are here with us. One of our werewolves runs into the room, he has a ghoul on his back, he is trying to free himself. I watch as the ghoul bites down on his neck. Suddenly my mind floods with the memories of the madness. I look at Camaz with fear in my eyes. He jumps in front of me, in a protective stance. Suddenly there is ghouls everywhere. I watch as two of them rush Camazotz. I scream out, "Look out, behind you!" He turns just in time, swings his sword, taking the head of one of ghouls, he swings around, catching the other in his chest. The beast screams out in pain, falling to the ground. Camazotz swings again, taking the ghouls head. All of a sudden, we are in battle, with four of them. The first two have knocked Camaz from in front of me, the other two rush me. I swing my sword taking the head of one of them, the other knocks me to the ground. I lose my sword. I quickly pull my daggers from their sleeves to fend off the creature. He is very strong, preventing me from striking. I can smell his foul breath as he lowers his head toward me. I begin to scream out, I know if he bites me, I will be lost in the madness forever. I see a steak of silver out of my eye and the ghoul is gone. It is Kimsu, he has come to my rescue. He has the ghoul on the ground, I watch as the ghoul bites him. I scream out "NO" then I am on my feet. I retrieve my sword, running at the ghoul, but before I reach him, Kimsu rips his throat out. I run up telling him how sorry I am, that he has been bitten by the ghoul. He smiles at me with all those razor sharp teeth and says, "Do not worry my lady, I am not affected by their bite." I think to myself, "Thank god!" I turn around looking for Camaz and our son. They are both in battle with a dozen ghouls. They are both moving so fast, it is hard to keep up with them. I run toward the battle readying for the attack, when I feel a sharp pain in my back. I turn coming face to face with the leader of the ghouls. I reach around and feel the silver spike sticking in of my back. I hear him say, "Now little vampire, you shall die and I will have avenged my brother's death!" He retrieves another spike from his belt, raises it, preparing to deliver the fatal blow. I close my eyes and cry out to Camaz in my head, "I love you!" I hear Camaz scream out, then there was darkness. As I float in the darkness, I am not afraid, I can feel Cassandra's present here with me. I with me. I hear her sweet voice, calling to me, asking me to wake up. I open my eyes and stare into Camaz's beautiful emerald green eyes. I say, "Have I died and gone back to heaven? I did not think I would ever get to see you again my love. I am sorry that you had to die as well, but at least we are together in our afterlife." He smiles down at me and says, "My dear, I am not dead and neither are you!" I look at him odd and ask, "Then where are we?" "You are safe my queen and in our quarters I have bleed into your wounds and you are healing quite nicely." I ask, "What happened? All I remember is the ghoul stabbing me in the back, and swinging the other spike at my heart." "You where very lucky my dear, you managed to bring your hand up, as he was delivering the blow, the spike went through your hand. But did not reach your heart. I destroyed him before he could swing at you again." I say, "Where is Camazotz? Is he safe?" "Yes, my queen, he is quite well. I am so proud of our son! He has become a mighty warrior and will make a wonderful King! He is with Michelle right now. Would you like to see them?" "Yes, please." Camaz calls for our son and they enter the room. He comes up to me, smiles and says, "Oh Mother, I am so glad you are okay! I did not think I would make it to you in time. But then I saw father go after the ghoul, with a vengeance!" I smile up at him and say, "I am so glad you are all safe. You know I would have laid down my life to save any of you!" "I know you would Mother and I would have gladly done the same!" Michelle comes up to me, kisses me, on the forehead and says, "I am so happy you are doing better, we all were so worried about you!" "Thank you child." Camaz says, "Okay, your Mother needs her rest, you can come visit her again later when she is feeling better." So the two of them leave the room. I ask Camaz about Kimsu, he tells me that he is recovering

from his wounds and would be fine. He says, "Are you hungry

my dear?" "Yes, as a matter of fact, I am starving!" "Then I shall

go get your dinner, I will be back in a few minutes." He then

leaves our room. I lay in the bed thanking our god for being alive.

I hear her sweet voice in my head saying, "You are quite welcome

my child." As promised, a few minutes later, Camaz returns with

my meal. He lays the man down beside of me and says, "Drink

my love, so that your can return to me, in all your glory." I move

the man's head to the side, strike and begin to drink him down.

His sweetly evil blood gives me strength with each drop. Once I

have finish, Camaz picks up the lifeless body and removes it from

our room. He returns to me, sitting down on the bed, pulling me

up into his arms, kissing me tenderly. God how I love this man!

CHAPTER 24

RETURN TO JAMAICA

A few weeks later, I have fully recouped from the ghoul's attack. We are out hunting one evening when Camaz asks, "So my love, where would you like to go for our Anniversary this year?" I think to myself for a minute and answer, "I would love to go back to Jamaica!" "Then that is where I shall take you!" A week later we are on our island off the coast of Jamaica. Camaz picks me up into his arms and carries me into the house he and says, "Welcome home to our island paradise my beautiful queen!" He sets me down on my feet, I stare up at him and say, "Thank you! I have so longed for us to be here again and alone!" He says, "We must get ready for sleep my dear, daylight is coming quickly." I look at him and say, "I want to try something, we have exchanged blood many times now in this new body, I want to walk in the sun!" "But my love we do not know if it will work! I cannot chance losing you!" I smile at him, "I will know right away if it does not work, I promise I will come right back inside." So we go out onto the porch to await daybreak. As the sun begins to rise, I can feel the warmth on my body. Oh how I have missed that. Just then I feel something, it is a burning, but it is not unpleasant, I turn to Camaz and he gasps and says, "Oh my, there is my beautiful queen in all of her red glory!" I raise my hands in from of me and marvel at the glowing red skin. My heart begins to sing! I walk out into the sunlight, loving every minute of it! We go out to the beach and lie down in the sand. He tells me that he to had longed to walk in the sun again, but would not because I couldn't. So we lie there for hours enjoying the warmth of the sun. We go for a swim in the warm waters of the ocean, playing with all of the wonderful sea life. They do not fear us, as if they know that we will not harm them. That evening I told him that I wanted to go to the mainland for the hunt, but first I wanted to go into town to listen to some of the local music. I have always loved listening to Jamaican music. We arrived in town around 9p.m. and found a local out door cafe that had music playing loudly. We are seated at a table. The waitress asks us for our drink order. As I have said prior, we can drink other liquids besides blood. I order a rum and coke, he orders whiskey. As we sit there enjoying the local music we are approached by a local vampire. I can tell by his scent that he is a made vampire. He introduces himself as Lamarr we offer him a seat and he joins us. He begins to ask us questions about ourselves. We tell him that we are from Mexico here on vacation. We do not tell him about our island though. He tells us that the prey is very plentiful here and tells us all of the best spots for hunting. Soon we say goodbye to our new friend and head off into the beautiful Jamaican night in search of our next meal. A few minutes later we arrive in a seedy part of town. The scent of blood is heavy in the air. I let my sense of smell range out in search of the wonderful smell of pure evil. Soon I pick up something. I smile at Camaz and we take to the air. We land deep in the jungle and begin to track the scent. We come upon an encampment, there are any bad men here. From what I can tell, they are drug smugglers. I signal for Camaz to go around the other side of the encampment. I ready myself for the game. I smear dirt all over me and take one of my fingernails, opening up wounds on both arms. The blood begins to trickle down. I begin to walk out from my cover. I can hear Camaz in my head praising me for being such a cleaver woman. I stumble into there encampment and fall to the ground. One of them comes running up to me asking if I am alright. I proceed to tell him that I was attacked by a wild animal, out in the jungle, that I had gotten separated from the group that I was with. He looks at the wounds on my arms, I have done quite well they look like claw marks of some big cat. He is so close to me that he has set my throat ablaze! I can feel the blood lust building within me, but I will wait a little longer. It has been awhile since I have played this game and I want to enjoy myself for a bit. He helps me to my feet and takes me over to the campfire. He tells me that one of his men is a doctor and will be right back. While he is gone I take it all in. I have counted a total of four men and four women here, I alert Camaz to make ready for the attack. The man soon returns with the doctor, he looks at the claw marks on my arms and begins to dress them. Even though they are being very nice to me, I cannot forget what they are, I cannot spare any of their lives. I have become extremely thirsty, so the game is over. I knock the doctor to the ground, he looks up at me in disbelief and says, "Are you crazy! Why did you do that!" I say, "I am sorry but I am quite thirsty and your blood is calling to me!" I smile showing my fangs. He begins to scream, I can hear others screaming all around me, so I know that Camaz has attacked. But I do not have time for anything, the blood lust has taken over and has sent me into a feeding frenzy! I rip the man's throat out and begin to drink. God his blood is so, so sweet! Once I have finished him, I jump to my feet and set off after the others. I find one hiding in a tent. I tear through the tent knocking him to the ground, I rear back and strike. He is screaming the whole time. I finish him within seconds. Out I go, in search of more. By the time we are finish everyone is dead. I am sitting next to my last victim, Camaz comes up to me and says, " Well, my dear, that was quite fun, are you ready to go back to the island?" "Yes I am, but I have eaten so much, I do not know if I can get up from here!" He reaches for me, pulling me up into his arms. He carries me all the way back to our boat. As I sit there with the wind blowing in my face, I smile to myself. I can hardly wait till sunrise! We made love until the sun rose, and we went out and enjoyed the sun on our faces. afterward we went back inside to sleep. We awake just in time to watch the beautiful sunset and we make ready for another trip to the mainland. I look up to the night sky, there are so many stars shinning brightly up there and the moon is full tonight. God how I love the night sky! We soon reach the mainland, we take off into town in search of our prey. Camaz has picked up on a scent and I am following close behind. Soon we reach a small house on the outskirts of town. I can smell the evils inside. But I also pick up on the scent of a vampire, it is that of our new friend Lamarr. He lands in front of us and says, "Well hello there friends, we seem to be stalking the same prey!" I laugh and say, "That we are, but there is plenty to go around!" We all enter the house from a upstairs window, there are four men in the house, one is up here but the other three are downstairs. Lamarr goes after the man up here and we go downstairs. They are all in the living room watching a soccer game on T.V. They do not hear us enter the room. I clear my throat for them to hear and say, "So, what is the score boys?" They all jump to there feet, one of the men draws a gun from his waistband and says, "How in the hell did you get in here! Are you crazy, we will kill you!" I begin to laugh ,saying, "Why silly man , you cannot kill something that is already dead!" I smile at him.The look on his face was priceless! He fires his gun at me, the bullet hits me in my arm but does no damage. I leap at the man, knocking him to the ground. He tries to fire at me again, but I break his wrist, making him drop the gun. He screams out in pain and says, "Get off of me creature from hell!" I laugh and say, "Sorry, but I am not from hell, but that is where I am sending you!" I strike, sinking my fangs deep into his neck. His sweet blood begins to flow, I savor every drop. I stand up from his lifeless body, wiping the blood from my mouth. Camaz has taken out both of the other men. Just then Lamarr comes into the room saying, "My goodness, you two are quite the hunters!" We all laugh at and leave the house. We say goodnight to our friend, letting him know that we will be returning home the following evening. We have invited him to come for a visit and he tells us he might just do that sometime in the future. When we arrive back at the island, Camaz tells me that he has a great surprise for me, he goes into the other room. A few minutes later he returns with a large box with a big red bow on it. He says, "Happy Anniversary my darling!" He hands me the box. I remove the bow and open

The box, inside is the most beautiful sword I have ever seen. It has beautiful etching on the sliver blade and the hilt is solid gold, encrusted with emeralds. He tells me that he has had it made special order for me. He says, "Read the inscription." I look at the hilt of the sword, there in beautiful script, is the words, "My love, my life, my everything." I look up at him with tears in my eyes and say, "Oh Camaz, it is so beautiful! I love it!" He pulls me up into his arms, kissing me madly. We make love for hours that night and right before sleep. I hand him his present. He opens it and smiles at me. I have had a matching dagger made to go with the other one I gave him a few years back. I say, "Look my love, read the inscription." There on the blade were the same words he had inscribed on my sword. "My love, my life, my everything!" He looks at me lovingly and says, "Oh my queen, I love you with all of my heart! You are my one true love!" He takes me in his arms kissing me tenderly. A few hours later we are aboard our plane heading for home. God how I will miss the wonderful

Jamaican nights!

## CHAPTER 25

## WONDERFUL NEWS

The time had finally come for Camazotz and Michelle's wedding and crowning to be the next king and queen of our kingdom. Samuel and Kim were making plans to go on a long vacation, so that he could show her the world. We were all upstairs getting dressed. The gown that Maria had created for Michelle was almost as beautiful as mine. I told her how stunning she looked in it. She thank me and ask, " Did you like being queen?" "Oh yes my dear, you have no idea how much fun you are going to have! I can still remember the day I was crowned. Like Camazotz and yourself, his father and I where married and crowned on the same day." There came a knock at the door. I go to answer it and there is my handsome husband in all his glory. The pride is beaming from him! I have chosen the emerald green gown that I had worn the day I came back to him. He picks me up spinning me around and says, "Oh how I love this gown! My one true love, you look ravishing!" He gives me a quick kiss. He goes up to Michelle, takes her hand, kissing it and says, "My dear, I must say, you make a beautiful bride! Are you ready?" She smiles at him and says, "Yes, I am ready." He leads her from the room. Camaz will be walking her down the aisle, as her family thinks she was killed in a accident. As they enter the great hall, everyone stands and cheers. I watch as our son's face lights up at the sight of her. He smiles the most glorious smile I have ever seen. They reach him, Camaz takes her hand and places it into our son's. Then the ceremony began. Camaz returns and sits beside of me. They say their wedding vows and promise to love and protect each other for all of eternity. Astor pronounces them man and wife and our new king and queen. Everyone stands up and cheers for their new rulers. All of our friends and family are now assembled in the great banquet hall, awaiting our new king and queen. A few minutes later they enter the room, go to the throne, and take a seat. Camaz and calls the party to order. He raises his glass to toast the happy couple and says, "Once in a lifetime, you meet someone who is your soul mate, you feel this in your heart, because it makes it sing! I wish you both all of the happiness that I have had with my soul mate and that your love is as strong as ours has been." I smile up at him beaming the joy of his words. Camazotz. raises his glass to his bride and says, "My one true love, I have loved you from the moment I laid my eyes upon you and I promise to love you for all of eternity!" She smiles at him saying, "As I will love you my king!" They kiss and everyone cheers. Soon the party is fully under way. Everyone is dancing and enjoying the evening. As we dance around the floor Kimsu comes up and ask if he can have the next dance. Camaz then bows to him placing my hand in his, we begin to dance. While we are dancing he tells me, "Oh how I wish I could know such happiness! You two are so much in love." I smile at him and say, "Someday you will find your one true love, I know it!" We dance for a few minutes more, then return to our table. I sit down and tell Camaz that I want to discuss something with him later. He says, "As you wish my queen." It is now time for dinner, all of our prey has been released into the woods for the hunt. God how I love the chase! Once we return from the hunt and say our good nights to every one we retire to our quarters. Once inside Camaz says, "So, my dear, what did you want to talk to me about?" "I hate seeing Kimsu so alone, so I though we would begin a search for his kind." "Woman you never cease to amaze me! You have such a good heart! We will talk to the council tomorrow and have them begin a search all over the world." He pulls me to him saying, "But right now, I have something else in mind!" He begins to kiss me. I can feel the fire begin to build way down low. I break our embrace and say, "Would you like to join me in the bath my love?" I walk into the bathroom, removing my clothes as I go. A few minutes later I sit in a hot tub, with my back to him, resting my head on his chest. He takes the sponge and begins to wash my arms. I love when he washes me, it so excites me! He runs the sponge down my neck kissing right behind it. I grunt with passion as he kisses my neck. He laughs and says, "My, my, what was that my dear? Are you trying to tell me something?" He licks from the base of my neck all the way back up to my ear. This pushes me over the edge! I turn around to face him, look him deep in his eyes and say, "Now my love, my need is great!" He picks me up and carries me from the bathroom. He lies me down on the bed. Then he starts to kiss and lick my neck again, he knows that this drives me wild. I begin to moan with delight and he raises himself above me, looking down at me he says, "My queen, you are so hot, I can feel the heat coming off of your body! Your scent is driving me wild!" I pull at him saying, "Please. Please. I need you!" He lowers himself and enters me. I scream out in delight over and over until he brings me. dig my fingernails into his back causing him to scream out in pleasure. He releases himself at the same time I do. We lie there panting, it still amazes me, that even as a vampire, I can get out of breath! The pleasure is still rocking my body with little shivers that run up and down my spine. He rolls over on his side stroking my face, saying, "Woman you are amazing! Never in my wildest dreams, did I know, when I first met you, that you would give me such pleasure!" I smile at him and say, "The pleasure was all mine my king!" He chuckles at that and pulls me to his arms. There I fall off to sleep smiling. The following evening when we awoke he asks, "Where would you like to dine tonight my love?" I smile and say, "I was thing about country food, I am in the mood to run!" A few minutes later we are running full speed through the woods. As usual I am trying to catch him. Then something strange happens, I catch up to him! We tumble to the ground laughing all the way down. He says, "Finally, you have caught me my queen!" I laugh and say, "I caught you a long time ago, my one true love!" He pulls me to his chest and says, "That you did, body, heart and soul!" He then kisses me passionately. A few minutes later we are up running again but this time I am right by his side. Suddenly the wind shifts and I pick up a scent. I stop testing the air. I say, "There, off to the west, something delicious!" We head off in that direction. We take to the trees and look down on a man, he has a woman up against a tree, ripping at her clothing I leap from the tree landing on the ground next to them. I startles the man, he steps away from the woman. Just then I catch her scent, she is the evil not him! I can tell by the pure evil in her blood that she has loured many men in this way to their deaths. The man yells at me to go away, that this is his party. I tell him, "No, sorry, but this is my party, I suggest you get out of here, I do not wish you any harm, it is her that I want!" I then bare my fangs at him. I watch the horror build in his face. He takes off running. The woman screams at me, "What right do you have to run him off! I was just starting to have fun!" I turn the the woman and say, "Oh but we are still going to have some fun, you have been a very bad little girl and I am here to punish you for all that you have committed!"

I leap at the woman, knocking her to the ground. I straddle her and say, "Now hold still, I am starving!" She begins to fight me, like a wildcat, this is making her heart pump faster and faster in return it ignites the blood lust in me. I have had enough of her puny attempts to fight me off. I slam her head to the side and strike. She screams out in pain as my fangs puncture her neck. I feel her blood begin to flow into my mouth. I drink her down, enjoying every drop. I release her lifeless body. Stand, looking to the trees. I see my beloved just standing on the branch where I left him. He leaps down to join me and says, "Well my dear, I must say that was quite enjoyable watching! Did you enjoy yourself?" "Oh yes, she was oh so sweet!" He takes my hand saying, "Lets hunt, I am so hungry!" So off we run in search of his meal. It doesn't take him long to pick up on the scent of his prey, I watch as he gracefully stalks his dinner. I love to watch him hunt, it is so hot! Soon he comes upon a man in a field. I watch as he leaps to a tree right above where the man is standing. I can smell that sweet scent of evil coming off of his body. It sets my throat ablaze. But I stay back, this is his meal, as I have already had mine. I watch as he leaps from the tree branch like some sleek cat, landing on his prey, knocking him to the ground. I watch as he begins to feed. This causes an even greater burn to start way down low! God he is amazing! He stands up from his prey, looks my way and smiles. Then just as quick he is by my side. He pulls me into his arms and kisses me. After a few minutes I pull away from his lips and say, "I so love to watch you hunt! Do you have any idea how it turns me on?" He gives me a beautiful smile and says, "Are you trying to tell me you are in need of something my queen?" I pull him back to my lips and show him just what I am in need of. We tumble to the ground ripping at our clothes until we are completely naked. He stares down at me and says, "God, you are so beautiful! You are my heart, my love, my life. I will love you for all of eternity!" I pull him down to me, kissing him madly. I feel him enter me and I scream out his name. We made love under the beautiful night sky for hours, then just laid there staring up at the moon and stars. I smile and say, "God how I love the night! I have never been so happy, thank you for this wondrous live my love!" "It was my pleasure, my beautiful queen!" We get up, dress and head back home. That night I dreamed of our first meeting when I was still human. What a wonderful dream! But something happened in the dream. I am looking off toward the mountains and I can see the darkness coming, I begin to run, but it is catching me. I begin to scream over and over for help. I am engulfed in the darkness. I cannot hear, see or feel anything. Suddenly I hear a voice off in the distance, it is calling my name. I try to follow but to no avail. I know the voice is that of our god Cassandra. I begin to pray for guidance and I here her voice in my head. "My dear child, I have come to warn you, there is a great darkness coming to your lands. You will be tested to your very limits. But I have faith in you, as you are one of my chosen ones." I ask, "What is coming?" "This is all I can tell you for now my child, but the great darkness will involve the human race." With that I wake up screaming, Camaz garbs me and shakes me the rest of the way awake. He says, "I am sorry dear, but you where having a nightmare!" I look at him with blood tears streaming down my face and say, "We are all doomed, the darkness is coming for us!" I proceed to tell him of my dream and what Cassandra had warned me of. He says, "But how can the humans pose a threat to us? They do not even believe in our existence!" "I do not know my love, maybe it has something to do with the hunters, maybe they are going to expose us." He gets up saying, "Come let us dress, we need to go to the council to alert them of this!" Once we have dressed we head for the council's chambers. Once there we tell them of my dream and Cassandra's warning. Astor lets us know that they will send out warnings to all of the kingdoms to be on alert. Also, we will begin a massive search and destroy mission on the vampire hunters. Once we are back in our chambers I ask him, "Camaz the hunter's are all innocents, how can we kill them if they are not trying to destroy us? We have taken a blood oath to protect all innocents!" I can still remember how I reacted to the hunter I had killed. He says, "My love, I understand your concern, but if it is the vampire hunters that will be our down fall, then we must do anything in our power to stop them!" A few days later we receive word that a group of hunters consisting of doctors and scientists have been experimenting on captured vampires and have learned how to put us in the darkness. They are located in a remote area of the Congo. We alert everyone to make ready for the trip, we must stop these madmen before the can release the virus on our world! We arrive in the Congo a few hours later. We begin our search for the hunters, it will be very hard to find them since they do not smell of evil. I am still not happy with the idea of killing innocent humans. But I must to protect all of vampire kind. We have had our friends in the Congo searching for the headquarters of the hunters. They have gotten a lead and now we are headed that way. The sweet blood of the innocent fills the jungle air setting my throat a blaze. But we have to be careful that we take out the right humans. We follow the mighty Congo river deep into the jungle and we come upon a large compound. The smell of human blood is overwhelming. There are guards stationed all around the compound with strange looking weapons. Camaz points up and we take to the air high above the compound so that the humans cannot see us coming. We survey the area looking for the entrance to go inside. There are two men atop a well guarded building so we assume this is where the scientists are located. We swoop down quickly, taking out the two men atop the building before they can fire their weapons snapping their necks like twigs. We will not drink from any of these men knowing what the blood oath will do to us. We look for away into the building. We enter through a air shaft and descend down in the heart of the building. We reach a large area and stare at all of the scientific equipment below, there are many men below. They are loading something into the strange looking weapons we had seen earlier. In all there are 10 men and 2 women below us. I watch as one of the women begins to leave the room. I tell Camaz that I am going after her, that I am going to kill her and take her clothes, I will return to the room like I am one of them. I go back into the shaft and find an opening, I look around to make sure there is no one there. I open the grate and leap to the floor. I hide behind a door as I hear her approaching the room. As she enters the room I slam the door behind her and leap on her, knocking her backwards She hits the floor hard and begins to scream. I place my hand over her mouth and snap her neck. I pull her lifeless body into a closet, remove her clothing, and dress in them. I come out, pull the door closed and break it so that no one can open it. I make my way back to the room where the men are at. I use the woman's badge to open the door, and walk in. As approach the men one of them comes up to me and says, "Hello there, I have not seen you here before you must be new." I smile at him being careful not to show my fangs and say, "Yes sir, I just arrived a few minutes ago, my name is Doctor Anne Camaz and may I ask your name?" I love playing this game! He replies, "I am doctor Jonathan Campbell and I am very pleased to meet you!" I can see the lust in this man's eyes so I know I have him right where I want him! I say, "So, Dr. Campbell, can you catch me up to speed on the production of the virus. I am so ready for them all to be gone from our world!" I am flirting with him the whole time, I hear Camaz's voice in my head saying, "Well done my queen!" The man proceeds to tell me all that is going on. I am quite appalled at what he is telling me. They have used our kind in their research to find out about the darkness and now they ave produced a virus that will plunge any vampire into the darkness forever! All of the research and the virus is locked away in the vault below. They are planning to start the attack in a few days! All the while he is talking I am relaying all this information back to Camaz. I say to him in my head, "My god, he is a madman, we have to stop them and destroy everything before it can be released on our world!" This man is the one who invented the virus so I need to take him out as quickly as possible. I know that he lusts for my body, so I begin the game. As we are talking I brush my hand lightly across his. He looks at me. I give him my most seductive look ,without showing my fangs. He says, "My god, you are so beautiful! Do you have anyone that tells you that?" I answer, "No, I have been alone for a very long time. I lost my husband a few years back." "What a shame, someone so lovely should not have to be alone!" He reaches up to stroke my cheek, I do not pull away and allow him to touch me. He says, "My goodness, your face is cold! Shall we go somewhere else a little warmer?" I smile to myself thinking, "Hook, line and sinker." I respond, "Yes, that would be nice, it's quite cold in here." He stands saying, "Come we will go to my quarters and I will order us some dinner." A few minutes later we are in his quarters. As we enter the room I survey the area. There are three rooms in all, the living-room, kitchen and bedroom. He tells me to have a seat and he will get us some drinks. A few minutes later he returns with two glasses of whiskey. He hands one to me and says, "I hope this is alright, it is all I have." I tell him it is fine and take a sip. I set the drink down on the table beside of me and turn to him. I can see the lust building in his eyes. I say, " You are very sexy, would you like to have some fun?" He pulls me to him, beginning to kiss me. All of sudden he says "Ouch" and pulls away from me saying, "Hey you bit me, take it easy!" I smell and see the blood trickling down from his lip. This sets my hunting instincts ablaze. I can taste his sweet blood on my lips. I smile at him showing my fangs. He backs up and says, "Your a vampire! How in the hell did you get in here! Our compound is very well guarded!" I say with a smirk on my face, "Not as well guarded as you thought!" I plunge for him, he screams for me not to kill him. I now have my hands around his throat saying, "Why should I spare your life! It is you, that created the virus and planned my kinds total destruction!" I snap his neck. The blood lust has now taken over me completely. The hunger is driving me wild. I rear back to strike. but Camaz stops me saying, "No, my dear, you cannot drink, he is an innocent his blood will sicken you to the point you will not be able to help." I hold my breath saying, "I need to get out of here!" I leap to my feet and run from the room. Once outside of the room I regain my senses. I tell Camaz that I have learned where the research and virus is located. Our elite squad is busy handling the other humans here so we head to the lower levels where the vault is located. We reach the vault but there are many humans here all armed with the strange weapons. I pull my sword from my back, and charge at the two men in front of the vault, Camaz has done the same and is going after the other two. One of the men takes aim at me and fires. I leap into the air causing him to miss me, I come down with my sword and cut him across the neck almost severing his head. He falls to the ground and bleeds out. I quickly take out the other man before he can fire. I turn just in time to see one of the men Camaz went after fire his weapon. I scream out his name as I watch what ever has been fired, strike him in the chest. He goes down screaming out my name, and he lays there silent. I scream out "NO" and run at the man that fired at my beloved, swing my sword and decapitate the man. I run over to Camaz, I try to reach him with my mind, but he is not answering me! I begin to plead to our god, "Please, Please, Cassandra, do not take my beloved from me! I do not know what I will do without him, he is my whole life!!" I hear her sweet voice, "I am sorry child, but there is nothing I can do for him. Only he can pull himself from the darkness. But you need to go and destroy everything so this will not happen to any more of our kind!" I begin to cry uncontrollably, my heart is breaking! I have lost my one true love! I stand from Camaz, go over to the vault ripping the door from it's hinges. I walk inside and there are thousands of vile of the virus along with all of the research. I go over to were all of the research is located, remove all of the files and dump them onto the floor. I cannot break the vile while I am inside or the darkness will get me as well. So I set fire to all of the files. Replace the huge metal door, but leave it ajar just enough for the fire not to go out. I run over to my beloved's body, pull him up into my arms and run from this place. Once outside I take to the air heading back to where our plane is located. All of a sudden I hear a loud explosion, I look back at the compound just in time to see it destroyed. I think to myself, "Good! Now they will no longer have the means to destroy us." But my heart is breaking for I have lost my one true love! I arrive at the plane, all of our elite has returned and we make ready for take off. I take my beloved down below to our quarters, lay him on our bed and collapse on him, sobbing. I raise from his body with anger in my heart. The hunters better watch out, because "Death's Deliverer" Is coming for them!

# FROM THE AUTHOR

I am sorry for the cliffhanger, but I promise things are going to get much better for Anne in book 3 "Death's Deliverer". Follow her as she fights the Devil for her very soul and tries to become reunited with her one true love. Below is a sneak peak into her continuing story. I will be releasing "Death's Deliverer" by the end of this year.

52720157R00126

Made in the USA
Charleston, SC
25 February 2016